LOVE & SNOWBALL FIGHTS

A CHRISTMAS VALLEY STORY

J.R. LOVELESS

CHAPTER 1

ALIGHT snow fell outside the window of the warm, crowded bar and restaurant Lane Freeman worked for. He picked up a bin and made his way over to clear off a table its occupants had just vacated. Christmas loomed close, a mere three days away. Colorful lights were strung up on the eaves of the houses, and decorations were scattered on the lawns of the small town he'd lived in for the past six months. The holiday always reminded him of the things he didn't have: a home, family, or even friends. He didn't wake up with eagerness on Christmas morning or expect to find loved ones gathered around the tree when he exited whatever bedroom he currently slept in. There were no gaily wrapped presents or affectionate embraces, no cheerful laughter or tender smiles. Not anymore.

After his parents were killed in a car accident when Lane was fifteen, he bounced from foster home to foster home until his eighteenth birthday when he was no longer a ward of the state. After that he'd moved from place to place, worked whatever odd job he could find. Now twenty-three, Lane found himself in a place where the people all knew one another, a town called, ironically, Christmas Valley, Washington. He ended up there accidentally after hitching a ride from a long-haul trucker. The man left him behind, most likely because of the painful silence Lane brought in his wake with his inability hold a conversation outside of one-word answers. Since then he'd found a job busing tables at Tal's Bar and Restaurant, the only job available that Lane felt qualified for as he wasn't exactly a chatterbox.

Socially awkward and embarrassingly shy, he found it hard to talk to people, which made it difficult to be a waiter or make friends, harder still to meet a significant other. The only things Lane had were a three-legged cat named Chloe—a stray he'd found in the alley out behind the restaurant—and a tiny apartment over an elderly woman's garage.

"Lane!" his boss, Talbot Jenkins, shouted over the din. Tal was the epitome of kind and always made sure Lane had something to eat, especially after Lane had almost collapsed one night from hunger after starting work. He'd hired Lane despite his problem with talking to people. Over the six months, Tal had spent time trying to pull him out of his shell, and now Lane could hold a conversation without it being too stilted or full of long, awkward silences.

Lane turned to look at his boss from where he had begun to wipe down the table. Tal waved at him, motioning him over. Swallowing hard, Lane set the rag down in his bin and picked it up, weaving through the tables and patrons to the bar. Tal stood there with a man who looked a lot like him. As Lane approached them, he noticed how attractive the man was. Black hair framed a ruggedly tanned face with eyes gray as a steel pillar; his muscular body was lovingly hugged by a black T-shirt and well-washed blue jeans. He towered over Lane by almost a foot.

"Lane, this is my brother, Trey," Tal introduced him. "He's going to be helping out around here for a few days. Just wanted to let you know since you come in early for prep and he may be here."

Unable to meet Trey's gaze, Lane nodded and gave an uneasy smile before walking away. He caught a word from Tal as the music hit a lull. "…shy."

Continuing with his work, Lane forgot about Tal's brother until the place had emptied out and he started clearing the last of the tables. He was reaching for a glass when someone brought a hand down on top of his. He started in surprise and glanced up to see Trey standing there, bin in hand as well. Dropping his gaze, Lane yanked his hand away and darted off to the next one. His chest felt tight and he had no idea why his cheeks were flushed.

"How long have you worked for my brother?"

Trey interrupted his thoughts, causing him to almost drop a glass. People tended to avoid talking to him once they realized how bad his shyness really was. It left people uncomfortable and they didn't like to be uncomfortable. Lane chose to remain quiet and shrugged, placing a plate of chicken-wing bones into his bin, then wiping down the table. Tal had already disappeared into his office to go through the day's receipts, and the waitresses had all gone home for the evening, leaving Lane to do the cleanup. He didn't mind, really, preferring to do his work in the soft silence of the establishment after the doors were locked.

"You don't know?" Trey asked.

Lane had to clear his throat in order to answer this time, as it seemed obvious Trey didn't intend on letting him be. "Six months," Lane rasped.

"How'd you end up in Christmas Valley?"

Shrugging again, Lane fidgeted and rushed to clean up another table. Why didn't Trey seem to understand he didn't want to talk? When he didn't answer, it seemed to only prod Trey into continuing to talk.

"My brother and I were raised here, actually. Our father worked for the factory off Route 9 and our mother ran a dress shop for years before the Internet made everything easier to get hold of at a cheaper price."

Lane shivered as the rough tenor trickled over him, bringing awareness in a way he hadn't felt in a long time. If things weren't already a challenge for him, being gay made it worse. The only experience he ever had with another guy was a foster brother in one of the many homes he resided in over his three years in the system, a teenager named Gregory. They bonded rather quickly and Lane practically hero-worshipped the boy, who was a year older. Gregory took the time to get to know Lane and drew him out of his shell, making him feel special. Lane had no idea now if Gregory had done it just to get into his pants or if Gregory had really cared for him. Once the foster parents found out what they were doing, they immediately removed Lane from the home and he didn't see Gregory again until after they were released from the foster care system, a memory he didn't care to think of right then.

"I never wanted to stay here and got out as fast as I could, but Tal loved it. Moved back home after college and opened the restaurant." Trey hefted his full container and set it on the bar. "Are you planning on sticking around for good?"

Lane had the sense Trey wasn't asking for himself, but rather because he didn't trust Lane. "I don't know," he murmured and lifted his bin to head into the kitchen.

Trey followed. "Really? No long-term plans, then?"

Discomfort rattled Lane and he set his tray down near the sink harder than he intended. His hands shook as he picked up the dishes and began rinsing them off to put in the dishwashers. When Trey suddenly crowded closer, Lane let out an embarrassing squeak. Heat suffused his face and Lane bent almost in half over the sink trying to get away from Trey.

Trey brought both hands down onto the edge of the counter, effectively trapping Lane in place. "If you're here to hurt my brother or steal from him, you better think twice, you got me? He's had enough of your type coming in here and robbing him blind or leaving him with a mess to clean up."

Lane bit his lower lip, his breath shallow and thin. "I-I'm not."

"Not what?" Trey demanded.

"Not going to steal," Lane managed. He flinched when Trey raised one hand, believing the man intended to hit him, only to jerk when Trey gripped his chin in an uncompromising hold and forced him to look up at him. Trey glared down at him with steely gray eyes, silent and dangerous. Lane swallowed hard and tried to pull away. He could feel his chest getting tighter and hoped he wasn't about to have a panic attack.

Trey searched his face for several long seconds and then released Lane, stepping back. "You better not or you'll be answering to me. You don't fool me for an instant with this shyness bit."

He had no idea what he'd done to piss him off, but Lane didn't wait around for Trey to attack him again, instead darting around Trey and out into the front, racing for the bathroom. He barely made it to the toilet, throwing up the little bit he'd eaten earlier. His insides heaved with each retch and Lane found himself shaking once he finished, sinking to his knees and wrapping his arms around his waist.

Foster homes weren't always nice. There were a few where Lane had wondered if he'd make it out alive or not sometimes. The parents were drunks or violent by nature, hiding it well whenever the social workers came around, threatening to beat the hell out of any of the children who might rat them out, and wanting nothing more than to claim the check from the government for the ones they housed and rarely fed. Trey reminded him of those times.

By the time he exited the bathroom, the remainder of the cleanup was done and Trey was nowhere to be seen. Lane felt bad at not having finished his job on his own and hoped Tal wouldn't get mad. He clocked out, retrieved his jacket from the employee area, and silently exited the back of the restaurant to begin his short walk home. The streets rolled up rather early in the small town, most businesses closing by six in the evening, and there were only a handful of cars that drove by in the walk to his apartment.

Trudging up the stairs on the side of the garage, Lane wondered if maybe his time here was over. Maybe he should move on after what happened with Trey. He didn't want to cause any trouble for Tal, and he didn't know if he could be around Trey for however long he planned to stay. He frightened Lane.

Chloe met him at the door, purring and rubbing against his leg. Lane gave a tired smile and bent down to pick her up, hugging her briefly while allowing the door to close behind him. Tears stung his eyes and he fought them back. "Hi, Chloe," he greeted gently. "How's my girl? Are you hungry?"

Chloe meowed and butted her head against his nose, causing him to laugh. He carried her to the teeny kitchenette and set her on the counter. He grabbed a container of wet food and popped it open, then dumped the contents into her bowl. "Here ya go, baby." She dove in and Lane smiled, petting her back while she ate. "I hope your day was better than mine," he murmured.

Once she finished, Chloe sat down and began grooming herself, still purring. She was a beautiful black color with a white chest and two white feet. Her pink, heart-shaped nose twitched as she cleaned her face and paws.

Lane removed his jacket and hung it up on the hook behind the front door before he toed off his boots. He shed his clothing and tossed them haphazardly at the laundry basket. He could just make out the sound of the old lady's television set as he got dressed in a pair of pajama bottoms and a ragged T-shirt and wondered how she could possibly fall asleep with it so loud. Then again, he supposed she was rather hard of hearing.

He looked around the small apartment, at the yellow walls with white trim. A floral loveseat rested against one wall with an old cedar storage chest next to it, while directly across from both was a queen-sized bed. The only other piece of furniture was an entertainment unit nestled against the wall between the bed and sofa that held a twenty-seven-inch old-style television and some books. Lane didn't have many pleasures in life, but he did love to read.

The first thing he'd done after finding a place to live and a job to support him while he was in Christmas Valley was check out the local library. Borrowing books was the highlight of his week, sad to say, but he did rather get along with the librarian, a young woman named Vicky. She always had a new recommendation for him when he came in and seemed really kind. He would miss her and their weekly chats when he left.

Lane sighed and slid under the comforter. He reached up to snap off the lamp and lay in the darkness, ignoring the muffled sound of the TV nearby and staring at the ceiling. He tried to think of how he could have possibly angered Trey but could come up with nothing. Tomorrow he'd hand in his resignation and start packing up his things. Hopefully, Tal would let him finish out the week so he'd have enough money to begin fresh somewhere else. This time he would need to figure out how to travel with Chloe, never having had to worry about that before, but he couldn't leave her behind. He'd grown too attached to her now. Thankfully, he'd picked up a pet carrier three months back at a yard sale for five dollars, thinking it would come in handy to take her to the veterinarian for her shots and if she ever got sick.

He couldn't be sure how long it took for him to fall asleep, but when he did, his sleep was restless. He tossed and turned, facing off against Trey in his dreams only to find himself in Trey's arms. By the time his alarm went off, Lane had been through the wringer and he felt more tired than rested. If he wasn't convinced before, he was now. He couldn't stay. Not after this.

Chloe jumped up on the bed and meowed, cuddling up against him. Lane smiled sadly. "I think it's time we moved on, baby. We aren't welcome here any longer."

She gave a meow in response, tilting her head to the side. Lane scratched her under the chin and got out of bed, stretching with a light moan. He rummaged through the itty-bitty closet to pick out a pair of his jeans and a light green T-shirt for the day and then went to take a hot shower, ignoring the cold wood floor beneath his feet. The bathroom mirrored the rest of the apartment, small with yellow walls and white trim. Lane sometimes wondered who'd decorated the place before he moved in. He let the water heat up while removing his pajamas.

He didn't linger in the shower. Things were going to be hard enough when he spoke to Tal; drawing out how long it took to get to work wouldn't make it any easier. With a hand towel generously provided by his landlord, Lane wiped away the steam fogging the mirror and stared at himself. Slender, almost feminine features gazed back. His blond hair clung to his scalp, soaking wet, and his dull green eyes were ringed with dark circles, evidence of his poor night's sleep. He had no muscle to speak of, really, and his ribs were clearly visible. Someone who looked like Trey would never be interested in someone like him, even if Trey didn't hate him.

It pained him to know he cared so much about what a stranger thought. He was Tal's brother, though, and Tal mattered to Lane a lot. Lane looked forward to the time he spent with Tal during the morning prep work and even sometimes after the restaurant closed. Despite his reluctance early on, Lane now enjoyed his chats with Tal. Somehow Tal had even gotten him to open up about some of his past and the foster homes he'd lived in, including the ones he hadn't felt safe in. Tal didn't push or demand for more than Lane wanted to part with, but made Lane feel comfortable sharing the details with him. So knowing Trey thought he would take advantage or try to hurt Tal caused a deep ache in Lane's chest.

Sighing, he briskly towel-dried his hair and the rest of his body before getting dressed. He padded barefoot into the main room to put on his socks and boots. He fed Chloe and then pulled on his jacket.

"I'll be back later, baby girl," he said while opening the door.

Lane locked it and took the stairs carefully. He burrowed deep into his coat to try to ward off the bite of the wind. It was still a little early to report to work, so he stopped in at the Greasy Spoon, a diner everyone in town frequented for breakfast. Malia, one of the waitresses, smiled and waved at him. He waved back while scanning for a free place to sit. A stool was open at the counter and he made his way to it.

Malia bustled over with coffee. "Good morning, Lane," she greeted him enthusiastically as she poured him a cup.

"Good morning," he murmured.

"The usual?" she asked.

Lane nodded as he added sugar and creamer to his coffee.

He picked up his mug and took a small sip, giving a sigh of pleasure. It warmed his frozen insides.

"Scrambled eggs, wheat toast, and bacon coming right up," Malia said.

Lane had been too busy enjoying his coffee to notice the stool next to him was vacant. It wasn't until he heard "I'll have the same" in that rough tenor that he realized who'd taken the seat beside him.

Tightening his fingers on the mug, Lane ignored Trey and took another drink.

"Not going to say good morning?" Trey mocked.

Lane didn't respond. The heat of the coffee no longer warmed his insides. He felt colder than he had outside in the freezing wind. He kept his gaze locked on his coffee and huddled further into his jacket.

Trey made a scoffing noise. "Still playing the part, huh?"

Unable to stomach Trey's dislike of him, Lane stood and tossed down enough money to cover the coffee and food. He hurried out of the diner, ignoring Malia calling for him. There were knots the size of Alaska in his belly and he doubted he could eat even a bite of the eggs anyway. Had he come off as rude to Trey? Was that why he thought Lane wanted to take advantage of or hurt Tal? Maybe he should apologize. If he did, maybe he could stay in Christmas Valley. It was the only place he'd truly considered making a home for himself. Instead of quitting, maybe he could try talking to Trey first.

Lane made it to the restaurant and took out his key to unlock the back door. None of the waitresses had arrived yet and Lane breathed a sigh of relief at the silence, needing some time to gather himself. He started unloading the two dishwashers and getting the plates ready for the day, setting them within easy reach of the cooks. The saltshakers and the napkin holders needed to be refilled. Lane set out new sets of silverware on the tables along with paper placemats. He bustled from one end of the restaurant to the other, finding satisfaction in the mindless tasks.

Tal came in as Lane finished. "Hey, Lane. You're in a bit early, aren't you?"

Shrugging, Lane replaced the remainder of the placemats and cutlery back into their containers behind one of the service stations. "I didn't have any other plans."

"Did you at least eat?" Tal frowned.

He shook his head.

Tal gave him an exasperated look. "Let's go."

Lane followed Tal into the kitchen, knowing he wouldn't let him be until he'd eaten something. "Why didn't you eat?" Tal demanded as he took out a fresh piece of chicken and started up the grill.

"Wasn't hungry," Lane offered.

"We've had this conversation before, Lane," Tal huffed. "You aren't on the road anymore and you aren't in one of those damn foster homes. If you can't afford it, come to me. I'll help you out. You know that. I don't need you passing out on me again in the middle of work."

"I don't want you to use food from your restaurant on me. You never let me pay you back," Lane protested.

Tal glared at Lane. "It's my damn restaurant, Lane. I can do whatever I want. Now shut up and let me make you something to eat. Correction: tell me why you didn't eat while I cook."

"I really wasn't hungry."

"Bullshit, kid. Are you out of food again? Why didn't you stop by the diner on your way in? Do you need money?"

"No!" Lane felt cornered. He couldn't tell Tal about Trey or the real reason he didn't eat that morning, but he didn't want to lie to Tal. "I really wasn't hungry," Lane tried again.

Tal sighed as he set the piece of chicken on the grill and

turned to look at him. "I wish you'd talk to me, Lane. You aren't as alone as you think. I care what happens to you, buddy."

Discomfort set in and Lane fidgeted, playing with the belt loops on his jeans. "I know," he muttered, staring at the floor.

"Then stop giving me gray hairs!" Tal grunted. "Tomorrow morning I'm taking you to the grocery store."

Lane jerked his head up. "No! I-I don't want you to do that." Oh God, if Trey heard that, he'd think he was taking advantage of his brother even more. "I'll go myself."

Tal flipped the piece of chicken and gave Lane a skeptical look.

"I will, I promise!" Lane swore, almost begging.

"You better," Tal snapped. "Now do you want cheese on your sandwich?"

Lane relaxed, sighing quietly. "Okay."

The smell of the chicken cooking made Lane's mouth water and his stomach growl. The sound caused Tal to give Lane another agitated look, but thankfully he didn't say anything else as he finished preparing the chicken sandwich. Tal placed it on a plate and handed it to Lane. "Eat."

He accepted the dish and perched on a nearby stool before taking a big bite of the sandwich. He hadn't realized how hungry he was until he'd consumed the entire thing in minutes.

Tal cleaned up the grill while Lane ate and took the plate once Lane had finished. "Don't ever skip another meal, Lane. I mean it. You've put on weight since you've been here but you're still too skinny."

Flushing, Lane nodded and hopped off the stool. "I need to check on the bathrooms."

"No, you sit, let the food digest. I'll go check 'em."

"But it's my job," Lane protested.

Tal raised a brow. "And whose restaurant is this?"

"It's still my job," Lane replied stubbornly. "I should do it."

"And I'm your boss who is telling you to remain on that stool until the restaurant is ready to open, you hear me?"

Lane wanted to keep arguing, but when Trey stepped into the kitchen, he practically swallowed his tongue. He dropped his gaze to the floor and skirted around Trey, rushing out of the room.

Tal's voice reached him as he disappeared into the bathrooms. "What the hell did you do, Trey?"

As if Trey didn't have enough ammunition to hate Lane, now Tal thought Trey had done something to him. He didn't hear any more once the door closed behind him. He leaned against the counter, trying to breathe to calm his nerves, and struggled to keep the food down. A frown settled between his brows. How could he apologize to Trey if he couldn't be in the same room without wanting to throw up? That was going to be a real problem. Lane managed to get a tentative hold on himself and pushed away from the sinks to look in each stall. They were pretty clean. One of them needed a new roll of toilet paper, which Lane got from under the sink. After he replaced the empty roll, he cleaned off the sink with a couple of disinfectant wipes.

When he exited the men's room, he breathed a sigh of relief when he didn't hear Tal still yelling at his brother. He went into the ladies' room and did the same perusal. He swept up the loose paper on the floor and threw out some paper towels left on the counter. Everything else looked pretty good. Lane gave a nod of satisfaction and returned to the front of the restaurant. He ensured each table had been set and nothing was out of place.

"Lane?" Trey's voice came from behind him and Lane tensed, hands shaking.

He couldn't turn around to face Trey. Instead he chose to fidget with some menus, getting them lined up perfectly with one another. He almost jumped out of his skin and couldn't stop the small sound he made when Trey's hands came down on top of his, stilling his movements. Lane didn't know what to do. He flinched when Trey started talking.

"I'm sorry."

CHAPTER 2

LANE COULDN'T have been more surprised if his own parents had walked through the door of the restaurant right then. He wasn't even sure he'd heard right.

"I'm sorry," Trey repeated. "I'm so used to the people Tal hires taking advantage of how nice my brother is. He's had so many of them blow through here who stole from him, caused damage to the restaurant, and just used him for whatever they could. I tend to pass judgment before I get to know any new hires if they haven't been residents of Christmas Valley for a long time."

Lane tried to pull away from Trey, uncomfortable at the heat of Trey's hands on his. Trey didn't budge.

"I really am sorry. Will you please forgive me?"

Biting his lip, Lane hesitated and gave a short nod, trying once more to free himself from Trey. This time Trey let him go. Lane darted several feet away, still not looking at Trey, and wrapped his arms around his middle. He had to swallow multiple times before he could talk. "I-I care about T-Tal. I w-would never do a-anything to h-him."

"I know that now. I've never used my size or strength to intimidate someone smaller and I'm ashamed I did that to you. All I can do is ask for you to forgive me for being such a jackass."

Lane wondered what Tal had said to cause Trey to do such an about-face. Had Tal told him something or forced Trey to apologize? He looked at Trey from the corner of his eye for a split second. Trey really did look contrite. Taking a small breath, Lane whispered, "Okay."

Trey smiled and Lane dropped his gaze back to the floor. His stomach flip-flopped and he yelled at himself silently. Even if Trey didn't hate him anymore, it didn't mean he wanted anything to do with him.

"I'm sorry if I frightened you away from your breakfast this morning," Trey continued. "Will you let me repay you? I'd really like to make up for it."

Lane shook his head. "It's okay," he murmured.

"I insist. It's my fault you didn't eat."

Lane heard Trey move and then his boots appeared in front of him. He tightened his hands into fists, forcing himself to remain still. Strong, tanned fingers came into view grasping a ten-dollar bill. Surprise brought his eyes up to Trey. "This is too much," Lane protested.

Trey waved away his concern. "Take it."

Shaking his head, Lane tried to object again, only to suddenly lose the air in his lungs when Trey grabbed his wrist and pressed the money into his hand. Lane shivered at the callused skin against his. "I can't accept this," Lane managed.

"You can," Trey replied, releasing Lane. "It doesn't even come close to making up for what I did."

"B-but you d-don't have to," Lane stuttered. "It r-really is a-all right."

Trey grunted. "No, it's not, and I ought to slaughter the

asshole who taught you it was okay to be spoken to like that. You should have kicked me in the nuts last night."

Lane widened his eyes and furiously shook his head. "I would never do that!"

"Look at me," Trey said. When Lane kept his head bent instead of doing as Trey instructed, Trey repeated himself. "Look at me, Lane."

Drudging up the very small amount of courage in himself, Lane slowly raised his gaze to Trey.

"No one, and I mean no one, should ever be okay with being treated in such a way." Trey quirked his lips up in a slight smile. "If I ever do again, you have my permission to kick my ass, okay?"

Lane couldn't help but return the smile, a soft laugh slipping free. He nodded.

"Good," Trey said. "Now let's get to work, hmm?"

AFTER THAT an unspoken truce was called. Lane discovered Trey to be the kind of guy who liked to joke around and laugh, and his shyness at talking to Trey ebbed away. He found himself watching Trey whenever he could. At least when Trey didn't realize he was. By Christmas Eve Lane knew when Trey went back home, he was going to miss him. Which seemed rather ridiculous considering he'd only known him three days. Since Gregory, Lane hadn't allowed himself to become attached to anyone, and it disconcerted him to find he'd let his guard down around Trey. He didn't know how to stop himself from feeling the way he did either.

The weatherman called for a strong snowstorm to rip through the area over the next twenty-four hours. When the snow started falling at noon, Lane wondered if the other residents would be able to have their Christmas Day. He kept glancing out of the window throughout the afternoon. By the time it grew dark, the restaurant was dead and no one had come in for at least the last two hours. Lane leaned against the cold glass, looking down the street each way. Not even a single car came down the road. In fact, it had gotten so bad he could barely see the single stoplight they had in the center of town.

"It's really coming down out there," Trey said from beside him, startling him.

Lane nodded, placing his hand on the window.

"Tal wants to close up early. He sent the others home a while ago." Trey rested a shoulder against the wall, turning his body toward Lane. "I think you should stay in the room upstairs for the night, Lane. It's coming down too heavy for you to walk home. Tal and I are staying here too."

Lane shook his head. "I can't."

"I promise I won't bite," Trey said, eyes twinkling.

The thought hadn't even crossed his mind, but Lane shivered at the idea. What would it feel like if Trey did bite him? Somehow Lane knew he wouldn't mind. "I have to get home."

Trey sighed. "Why?"

"Chloe."

Lane saw Trey's reflection frown. "Who's Chloe?"

"My cat."

"Ah. I see. All right, wait here."

Confused, Lane looked over to see Trey walking toward his brother's office.

"Need to borrow the truck, Tal," Lane heard Trey tell Tal.

"Just make sure it comes back in one piece!" Tal shouted as Trey left, keys jingling in one hand.

Trey smiled at Lane. "Grab your things and let's go."

"I can walk!" Lane protested. "It's only a few blocks."

"You are not walking in that," Trey said, pointing out the window. "Now get your stuff."

Lane reluctantly did as Trey said and headed into the back room. He didn't know what he'd do being in such a tight enclosed space so close to Trey. His hands shook as he picked up his jacket. He pulled it on and zipped it up. Trey had pulled on his own coat and gloves by the time Lane met him by the door.

Trey frowned. "Where's your gloves?"

"I don't have any," Lane replied simply and stuffed his hands inside his pockets.

Trey heaved a sigh and started taking off the black leather ones he wore. Lane's eyes widened as he realized what Trey intended. "I'm fine," Lane insisted.

"Take them," Trey commanded, holding the gloves out.

"But you'll be cold!"

"I'll be all right. Come on, take them."

Lane tried to ignore him but Trey wouldn't let him. He yanked Lane's hands out of his pockets and stuffed the gloves into them. "Stop being so stubborn and put them on," Trey huffed.

Lane capitulated. They were quite a bit bigger than Lane's hands, leaving a lot of room to spare. Trey gave a satisfied grunt and opened the door, struggling to keep it from slamming against the concrete wall or closing on them. Lane could barely see Tal's truck sitting outside the door. He wondered if maybe it was a bad idea to be out in the storm, but he couldn't leave Chloe alone overnight, especially without feeding her. He fought through the snow and wind, reaching the truck and opening the door. A vicious gust almost ripped it out of his grasp as he climbed into the front seat. Trey joined him a few seconds later.

"Shit, this is bad!" Trey exclaimed.

"I'm sorry," Lane offered. "I can still walk."

Trey shook his head. "You aren't walking in this, Lane. Now which way to your place?"

"I live on Dasher Street."

Yes, the little town had thought it funny to name several streets after the eight tiny reindeer pulling Santa's sleigh. The longer Lane lived in Christmas Valley, the more he found the residents matched the town. They were quirky and nosy, but they cared about one another. At first, the townspeople coming through Tal's had seemed wary of him, but over the last couple of months they'd begun to accept his presence, even going so far as to smile and wave at him when they caught sight of him on the streets or in the local businesses.

Trey started the truck and Lane pulled on his seat belt. Trey followed suit and then put the vehicle into reverse, slowly backing out of the space and pulling out onto the street. Trey flicked on the windshield wipers, but even that could barely keep up with the snow. "Damn, I haven't seen one this bad in a long time."

The heater took several painful minutes to warm up. Lane sighed when he finally felt the hot air on his face. He leaned forward a tad, closing his eyes. All of his foster homes had been in southern California, so they never experienced weather requiring more than a sweatshirt or hoodie. In fact, this was Lane's first blizzard. He'd been in cold places over the last five years, but they never received a snowfall like the one they were in right then. The wind rocked the truck every few hundred feet. It was rather terrifying.

"How long have you had your cat?" Trey asked.

"Almost six months." Grateful for the distraction, Lane sat back in his seat and tried to see the house fronts they were creeping by out of the window. "I found her out behind the restaurant. She only has three legs. The veterinarian said she was born that way."

"Is she able to get around on just three?"

"Almost as well as a cat with four legs," Lane replied, smiling.

"Huh. That's pretty cool. I'd like to meet your Chloe some day."

"Sure!" Lane said. "She's a little wary of strangers, though. She may hide if she sees you."

The tires slid a little on an ice patch and Trey swore under his breath. Lane shuddered at the near miss. They were only half a block from his apartment when the truck hit another patch and swerved. Trey couldn't get it back under control and they skidded off the road, hitting a light pole and burying half of the front end in a snowdrift. Lane stared out of his passenger-side window at the pole, horrified at how close it was. He could just make out the buckling of the metal on the side of the truck where they hit it.

The impact, while jarring, wasn't hard enough to cause any injury. Lane still couldn't help feeling shaken from the situation. He glanced over at Trey, trembling.

"Shit!" Trey exploded, slamming his fist into the steering wheel and causing Lane to jump. He turned in his seat. "Are you all right?"

"I'm fine," Lane replied.

"Are you sure?" Trey demanded and reached out to run his hands over Lane's arms and legs, checking him over.

Lane sucked in a breath at Trey's touch. "I'm really okay," Lane managed.

Once Trey seemed satisfied with Lane's uninjured limbs, he tried to start the truck again, but all it did was make an awful churning noise. "Fuck, Tal is going to kill me!"

"I'm sorry," Lane said.

"Don't be. It's not your fault."

"If you hadn't been driving me home, you wouldn't have run off the road, though!"

Trey sighed and sat back, giving Lane an impatient look.

"I insisted, and no one could have known this would happen." He reached into his pocket then grimaced. "Damn. I forgot my cell at the restaurant. Do you have yours with you?"

Lane wanted to protest further about the accident being his fault but figured it wouldn't get them anywhere. "I don't have a cell, just a landline."

"How far is it to your place?"

"Just down the street from here."

"We're going to have to walk the rest of the way. After I get out, I want you to climb over and exit my side of the truck."

Nodding, Lane shivered when Trey opened the door, the cold quickly erasing the heat from inside the cab of the truck. Trey gave him a look before he stepped out and waited for him. Lane undid his seat belt and made his way over the console in the middle, almost catching his left foot in the cup holder. He held on to the steering wheel for a second, steadying himself. Trey reached in a hand and grabbed hold of his bicep, helping him out of the truck. The wind sucked away any vestiges of warmth still left in his body and Lane's teeth immediately started chattering. He burrowed into his jacket as best he could, but it didn't help.

"Which way?" Trey shouted over the wind.

Lane pointed and started fighting the gusts of air toward his place. Trey grabbed his wrist. Looking back at Trey, Lane gave him a confused look. Instead of responding, Trey wrapped an arm around Lane's shoulders and pulled him in close. Lane's heart tripped several beats before he could get his wits about him. Trey wasn't holding him for any reason except to keep them together and warm until they could get to his place. He led the way, continually sliding on the icy sidewalk, but Trey's grip kept him from falling.

When they reached the garage stairs, Lane let out a small

sound of shock when he saw the bottom couple of steps covered completely in snow. Trey urged him forward and Lane fought through the fresh powder. He struggled to get his keys out of his pocket and unlock the door. They stumbled into the apartment and Trey slammed the door behind them, flicking the lock back into place. Lane stood there for a few moments to gather himself and then he turned on the lights, shrugged off his jacket and Trey's gloves, and went looking for Chloe, uncaring of the snow he tracked along the way.

"Chloe," he called. "Come here, baby girl."

A sad meow came from under the bed and Lane dropped to his knees near the edge, peering underneath. She'd wedged herself as close to the wall as possible.

"Shh, it's okay, Chloe. I'm home." She meowed again and crept to him, close enough to where he could reach her. Lane pulled her out and hugged her tightly, petting her between her ears. "I know, girl."

He heard Trey moving around behind him and the sound of the phone being picked up. Then a swearword came from Trey. Lane turned to see Trey slam the phone back into the receiver. "The phone lines are out," Trey growled.

"I'm sure they'll be back on soon," Lane offered.

Trey shook his head. "No. Tomorrow is Christmas and they won't send a repair truck out until after, especially in a storm like this. It'll take days for the roads to be cleared enough for them to get through, anyway."

Lane swallowed hard. Trey would be stuck in the tiny apartment with him for days? "I'm sorry," he murmured again.

Trey gave him an exasperated look. "How many times do I have to tell you it's not your fault? Enough apologizing, okay?"

He nodded and then buried his face in Chloe's fur,

peering over when Trey didn't say anything else. Trey had shrugged off his jacket as well and placed it on the hook near the door before picking up Lane's from where he dropped it and putting it next to his, stuffing the gloves into one of the pockets.

He approached the two of them slowly and crouched down. "So this is the famous three-legged Chloe, huh?"

Lane smiled. "Yep. Isn't she beautiful?"

"She certainly is," Trey murmured and reached out to scratch her beneath her chin.

Lane was shocked at how easily she accepted Trey's touch and how her purring deepened. "She likes you," he said.

"What's not to like?" Trey replied with a wink.

His heart jumped into his throat and he had to fight to keep from blushing. Lane could definitely say there wasn't anything to not like about Trey. The hard body, gorgeous gray eyes, and flirty personality made a dangerous package. Lane cuddled Chloe closer, wishing Trey were petting him instead of his cat, then reprimanded himself for having such thoughts. They only led to heartache and pain. Hadn't he learned that the hard way already?

"I'm not sure how long the electricity is going to stay on. We should turn up the heat for as long as we can." Trey looked around and saw the radiator near the window. He frowned. "That's all you have? No fireplace?"

Lane nodded. "The lady I rent it from said they built the apartment a couple decades ago, and the people who owned the place before her didn't want to spend the money for a central air conditioner or what it would cost to add in the fireplace for such a small apartment."

"It'll have to do." Trey stood and moved over to turn the radiator on full blast. "Did you happen to catch how long they said this storm was going to last?"

"No," Lane replied, starting to feel scared. "I didn't think it would be this bad."

Trey must have picked up on his emotions and smiled, coming back to where he sat with the cat. "It'll be all right. We are just going to have to get familiar for a couple of days, is all. Nothing is going to happen."

Lane bit his lip and tried to control his fear. Trey had grown up here, so he had experience with storms like this. "Okay," he murmured.

"Good. Now let's see if there's anything on the news."

"The TV only gets like five channels," Lane said. "I never worried about it since I don't really like watching television."

Trey shrugged. "There should be at least one news station."

He turned on the set and flipped through the few channels, finding one with a lady standing in front of a screen and pointing. Lane grew even further agitated when the weatherperson said the blizzard would last at least another eight to twelve hours. For the first time, Lane felt happy Trey was there. If he'd had to go through this alone, he didn't know what he'd do. He looked at Trey to find a worried expression on his face.

"What's wrong?" he asked.

The look disappeared. "Nothing. Everything is fine. It may be a good idea to consider asking your landlady if we could stay with her tonight, though."

"No," Lane protested. "I can't impose on her like that. Besides, she's allergic to cats and I won't leave Chloe! She almost didn't let me keep her to begin with."

Trey eyed Lane for a few moments, appearing as though he might argue the point, but then gave a nod. "Okay. Let's start gathering all of the blankets you have, and it might be a good idea to change out of these wet clothes and into something dry."

Lane eyed Trey. "I don't have anything that will fit you."

Trey waved his hand. "It's fine. I didn't think you would. Why don't you go change, hmm?"

Standing, Lane set Chloe on the bed. "Is everything going to really be okay, Trey?" he asked quietly.

"I promise, Lane. Now go."

He hesitated for a moment and then grabbed a pair of sweatpants and a T-shirt from his closet. When he'd moved in, Mrs. Johnson, his landlady, had said he could use anything left behind by the previous tenant. There were quite a few sheets and blankets he had aired out and washed. "The blankets are in the chest by the sofa."

Lane went into his bathroom and closed the door, listening to Trey moving around as he shed his wet clothing and pulled on the dry ones. When Lane returned to the other room, Trey had removed all of the blankets and set them on the bed. Chloe had curled up on top of the stack. Lane smiled while moving to the counter to open a can of food for her. He emptied it into her bowl and set it on the floor near the fridge.

"Is this all of them?" Trey asked.

"Yes. Is it not enough?"

"It's fine. Do you mind if I take off my shoes?"

"Of course not," Lane replied, frowning. "You don't have to ask."

Trey shrugged and toed off his boots, picking them up and placing them near the door. "It's just the right thing to do."

Lane almost died when Trey stripped his sweater over his head. The heavy fabric pulled at the bottom of the T-shirt Trey wore beneath it, causing the shirt to ride up enough to bare Trey's stomach. A dark smattering of hairs trailed down into the top of Trey's jeans and the tanned skin rippled at Trey's movements.

Lane's palms started sweating and he felt extremely hot while his mouth seemed dry all of a sudden. He tried to chalk it up to the heat pouring out of the radiator but knew he was lying to himself. If anyone had asked him a week ago if he'd known or even dreamed of something like this happening, he probably would have laughed it off or thought the person nuts. Here he was riding out a snowstorm with the sexiest man alive, and it appeared as though they would be stuck in his apartment for at least a day or two. The idea seemed ludicrous, yet it couldn't be more real.

"…flashlights?"

He blinked at Trey. "What?"

Trey gave him a strange look. "I asked if you have candles or a lantern or even a flashlight."

"Oh. Uhm… I think there's some candles under the kitchen sink," Lane replied, fighting a blush at how simple he must look to Trey. "There's a flashlight in the drawer near the fridge."

"Good. We may need those."

The lights flickered as he said it. Lane rushed to find them. He set the three tall jar candles on the counter. "I haven't needed to get others. I didn't think I'd ever need them," he offered apologetically.

Trey waved his hand. "Don't worry about it. We'll get by with these. Hopefully we *won't* need them."

"If you're sure."

"Nothing we can do about it now even if I weren't," Trey pointed out. "So what brought you to Christmas Valley?"

Lane eyed Trey dubiously at the inane question. "Just happened that way. I was riding with someone who stopped to eat at the diner and I ended up missing him when he left."

Trey frowned. "That's messed up."

Lane shrugged and moved to perch on his bed, drawing one leg underneath him. "He didn't owe me anything. It's not like we knew one another. Besides, I think I made him uncomfortable."

"You were hitchhiking?" Trey demanded.

"Yeah."

"Do you know how dangerous that is?"

He knew all about the dangers. Tal had lit into him when he found out about it, making sure Lane knew everything that could have possibly happened to him. "Tal already told me," Lane said.

That stopped Trey from building up to the yelling he'd been about to start. The steam faded and Trey paced to the loveseat, dropping down onto it. "Don't ever do that again."

"I didn't have any other way to get around."

Trey stared at him. "You say it as though it were just a part of life."

"It is." Lane couldn't say it any other way. He'd never learned to drive.

"Not anymore," Trey growled, surprising Lane.

"When I leave here, I need a way to travel," Lane protested.

"Leave? Why would you leave?" Trey sat forward on the sofa. "Did something happen to make you want to?"

Lane tilted his head to the side quizzically. "It always ends up that way."

"Not this time," Trey rasped.

Before Lane could think of something to say, Trey's fear came true. The lights flickered again and then went out.

CHAPTER 3

LANE SHIVERED at the sudden darkness. "Trey?" he whispered.

"It's okay," Trey soothed and stood, making his way to the candles by the dim light from outside. Once he'd lit two of them, he left one on the counter and brought the other to the nightstand near Lane's bed. "I figured this would happen."

Trey returned to his seat on the couch. "How long have you been on your own?"

Lane tensed. He didn't like talking about his past. Tugging at a loose thread in the blanket on his bed, he considered what he should say. "A few years."

"Where are your parents?"

"Dead."

"I'm sorry," Trey murmured. "How old were you when it happened?"

"Fifteen."

"That must have been hard. Did you have any other relatives?"

Lane fidgeted. "No."

Trey must have realized he didn't want to keep talking about his past and changed the subject. "I saw the books on your shelf. You like to read a lot?"

Enthused by the new subject, Lane nodded vigorously. "Every chance I get!"

Trey smiled. "I'm a movie man myself."

"Oh, but the movies are never as good as the books," Lane argued, leaning forward a bit. "Well, almost never. I managed to see the Harry Potter movies last year while I was in Sacramento. They were fantastic. As close to the books I think as possible."

"Hmm. Never saw those. What are they about?"

For the next half hour, Lane went over the series about a magical boy who didn't know he was special and his fight against a wizard who wanted more than anything to destroy him. Trey listened, nodding and making "huh" noises at the right parts. When Lane trailed off, he blushed. "Sorry."

Chuckling, Trey replied, "I enjoyed listening to you talk."

"It must have been boring."

"Not at all. I will have to watch them once the power comes back."

Lane peeked at Trey, watching the shadows cast by the candlelight playing across the tanned features. "Really?"

"Maybe you can show me them sometime."

"Sure!" Lane exclaimed and then fell silent. He fingered the hem of his sweatpants as he asked, "Wi-will you tell me about your life here in Christmas Valley?"

"You really want to hear about that? It's not as though this place is the epitome of excitement."

"I'd like to hear."

Trey eyed him for a moment. "Okay. If you start to fall asleep, I quit."

Lane shook his head. "I won't!"

"Thirty years ago, on a night like this—"

"Come on, seriously?" Lane interrupted.

Trey laughed. "No, not really."

"Trey!" Lane groused.

Holding his hands up in defeat and chuckling harder, Trey continued, "I was actually born in summer in the middle of the day. Even from the minute I could walk, I didn't want to sit still. I think I gave my parents a harder time than I should have. Tal tried to keep me in line, but even he couldn't keep me from doing stupid things."

Lane had no idea how long Trey talked, but he listened, fascinated, to all of the stories about Trey getting into all kinds of trouble. He envied Trey having the freedom to do so many things, yet he wouldn't take that away from Trey for the world. No one should have to grow up the way Lane had. Trey described the wild parties he and his friends had thrown, the dirt biking and stunt jumps they almost broke their necks during, and how they even skinny-dipped in the nearby lake. He went into how he left for college and barely came home since, setting up residence in sunny Dallas, Texas, as a firefighter.

When Trey finally reached to how he'd come home to visit his family for the holidays, Lane commented, "It sounds like you had a wonderful childhood."

"I guess I did. I never really thought about it."

"Isn't your job dangerous?" Lane asked.

"It can be if you don't follow protocol. We get called out on a lot more accidents than actual fires, really."

They'd been talking for a while now and Lane could feel the chill creeping into the apartment. He glanced out of the window to see the snow still coming down in strong flurries.

Trey must have picked up on his concern. "We'll be all right, Lane."

"I know," Lane murmured.

He heard Trey get up and come toward him. Trey placed

a hand on his shoulder, squeezing gently. "It should be over in a few more hours. Once it's light out, we can come up with a plan to get to my parents' place until the roads are clear and the power is back on."

"I can't leave Chloe," Lane objected.

Trey sank down on the bed next to Lane. "We won't. I promise. We'll find a way to get all of us there. Okay?"

He glanced at Trey. "Okay."

"Good. Why don't we start getting the blankets spread out over the bed? I hope you're not too uncomfortable with the idea of getting a little more familiar with one another."

Lane didn't understand at first. He gave Trey a nervous look.

"We're going to have to share," Trey explained drily. When Lane sighed in relief, Trey mocked, "I see where your mind went, dirty bird."

"I wasn't—"

Trey settled the tips of his fingers on one hand over Lane's lips. "Relax. I was only teasing."

Lane felt tingles race through him at the intimate touch and jerked away, flushing.

Trey stood and motioned for Lane to copy him. "Grab Chloe for me, would you?"

Unable to meet Trey's gaze, Lane snatched up Chloe and held her to him almost like a shield as he watched Trey start layering the various sheets and comforters over one another. Lane couldn't even fathom how he would find the courage to spend hours cuddled under blankets next to Trey. He couldn't be more embarrassed right then. He didn't even know if Trey was gay! Trey didn't seem fazed by the idea of what Lane had thought originally. Did that mean Trey liked men? Lane dashed that thought right away. Trey was just a really nice guy and probably didn't hold any prejudice against others.

When Trey finished, he turned to Lane. "I don't think it's cold enough in here yet for us to bundle together now. If you're feeling chilly, why don't you climb in first? I'll wait awhile."

"Are you sure?"

Trey shrugged. "I tend to run hot."

"O-okay," Lane stuttered and moved around Trey to slide beneath the blankets, still clutching Chloe. He leaned his back against the headboard, getting comfortable while Trey returned to the sofa.

Trey kept up a steady stream of chatter for the next couple of hours as the storm raged on outside their little world. Lane started getting nervous again as the cold invaded the small apartment. The place didn't have a whole lot of insulation. He fell silent after a while, Chloe curled up beneath the blankets close to his side. His gaze kept straying to the window and the snow and ice hitting the glass.

"Lane?"

Shaking his head, Lane looked over at Trey, who'd moved to the edge of the sofa. "Everything okay?" Trey asked. "You went quiet on me."

He gave Trey a shaky smile but didn't answer, tightening his hold on the pillow he'd picked up at some point. Trey stood and came over to perch on the edge of the bed. "Care to scoot over?"

Lane didn't know why, but the idea of being so close to Trey no longer scared him. He nudged Chloe over and moved toward the other side of the bed. Trey settled his long length beneath the blankets. He rested his back on the headboard beside Lane. "You've never been through one of these before, have you?"

"No," Lane whispered. They weren't touching but Lane could feel the searing heat of Trey's body next to him. He twisted his fingers in one of the many comforters over him.

"It can be a bit frightening if you haven't experienced it before. I remember the first one I ever went through. I was five years old and my parents were calm as can be, but me, I wanted to curl up in my closet and hide until it was over. We bundled up together in the living room in front of the fireplace with tons of blankets and candles, and they kept me and Tal occupied by playing games. After a while it worked and I didn't even notice when the storm ended."

"That sounds nice."

Trey smiled. "It was. Don't get me wrong, these kinds of storms can be extremely treacherous if you aren't careful, but we're inside. It's never a good idea to be outside in one of these."

Lane winced. "I'm sorry," he apologized again.

"Stop. I understand why you wanted to get home. I'm just glad I could be here with you to help you."

He stroked Chloe's side. "I didn't want to leave her on her own. Being alone can be awful."

"That's something you know a lot about." Trey's words weren't a question.

Lane bit his lip. "Yeah."

"That is one of the best things about Christmas Valley. You're never alone for long." Trey chuckled. "I used to think it was rather annoying, but it can be nice to have. In a big city like Dallas, people tend to ignore one another and go about their business in the hustle of everyday life. Sometimes we forget to slow down and see what's going on around us."

Lane knew Trey meant well, but even though he'd lived here for six months, he was still alone. He'd always be on his own. No one wanted someone as awkward as him around.

"What did you like to do while you were growing up?" Trey asked.

"Read."

"That's it? You never played any sports or anything with your friends?"

Quirking his lips, Lane replied, "I didn't really have a whole lot of friends."

Trey made a small humming noise. "So how old were you when you had your first date?"

Lane didn't know whether to laugh or cry at such an inane question. Most people could honestly answer with an age. He felt ashamed at not being able to share such a common experience with Trey.

When he didn't answer right away, Trey prodded him, nudging him with his shoulder. "You fall asleep on me over there?"

"No."

"Touchy subject?"

Closing his eyes, Lane turned his head toward the opposite wall, thankful for the lack of illumination on his features. "Never," he mumbled.

"It's never a touchy subject? Or…." Trey must have realized what Lane was saying. "Look at me, Lane."

He kept his face averted.

"Look at me. Please."

Shoring up his nerves, Lane opened his eyes and rolled his head toward Trey. His breath caught when he saw the way Trey was staring at him. He couldn't say for sure what he saw in Trey's expression, but it made his stomach knot and sweat dampen his skin.

"Don't ever be ashamed of who you are. Not everyone experiences things at the same pace. Life happens as it is meant to. Okay?"

He didn't really believe Trey's words, but he nodded anyway.

"We should try to get some sleep. May have a long day ahead of us tomorrow."

Lane slid down, jostling Chloe, who let out a meow of disturbance. He patted her head under the sheets. "Sorry, baby girl."

The moment Trey moved into a supine position beside him, the muscles in Lane's belly quivered and he attempted to curl into a ball to avoid contact with the hard planes of Trey's body. He heard Trey sigh and then he slid an arm under Lane, yanking him closer into Trey's side. Lane let out a sound of surprise, too stunned to think about struggling for the moment. The chiseled power rippling beneath Trey's flesh overwhelmed Lane. His head rested naturally in the curve of Trey's shoulder and the scent of his skin tickled Lane's senses. A delicate shiver ran through him. For a split second, he gave himself the right to enjoy the feel of Trey against him.

When he reminded himself of how stupid he was being, he tried to pull away, but Trey held fast. Trey's breath disturbed the strands atop Lane's head as he spoke. "Relax, Lane. It is merely for warmth. I'm not going to hurt you."

Lane stopped struggling but held himself stiff. He couldn't forget Trey would be leaving after the holidays and getting attached to him was a really bad idea. It would make it even harder to be alone again. He heard Trey's breathing even out and wondered if Trey had really fallen asleep. Tipping his head back, he studied the ridges of Trey's face: unruly locks of hair lay across his tanned forehead, the dark lashes resting against strong cheekbones, a nose with a slight crook showing it had been broken at some point, full and firm lips so unlike the ones Lane had known in the past, and a cleft chin he would give anything to have the right to kiss. The thought sent warmth spiraling through him, causing him to twitch in discomfort.

"Go to sleep," Trey murmured in a husky tone.

He started, surprised. "I th-thought you were asleep."

Trey cracked one eye open. "I can't while you're staring at me."

Warmth suffused Lane's cheeks and he angled his head down so Trey couldn't see him. "I'm sorry."

Trey's chest rose and fell in a soft breath of air. "You apologize too much. I don't mind that you're looking at me, Lane. I just don't think it's a good idea when we're in the same bed together."

Lane pondered what Trey meant and immediately thought Trey had picked up on his attraction to him. He ignored the hurt at Trey's rejection. He berated himself for even being upset and once more reminded himself of the number-one reason he needed to get ahold of himself. Besides, the concept of Trey being interested in him couldn't be more of a joke.

"I wouldn't do anything to you," he rushed to say.

A slight laugh rasped from Trey. "I'm not worried about you. I'm more worried about what I'd do to you."

Wait, what? Lane's eyes widened and he glanced up at Trey. Both of Trey's eyes were open now and Lane could clearly see the lust burning in their steel-colored depths. He'd encountered enough lecherous men during his hitch-hiking to recognize the emotion quite well. More than one had tried to make him pay for his travels with sex. He would never compare Trey to one of them, though, not by a mile. His mouth instantly dried out and his breathing grew shallow. Trey wanted him? He licked his lips, only to watch as Trey's eyes darkened. "I...."

"Now go to sleep," Trey growled low.

Lane scrunched his eyes closed, needing time to think. Good God, what did he do with that information? Trey desired him. It seemed too unfathomable to believe. Why would someone who looked like Trey, someone kind and amazing like Trey, want him, a skinny little nobody?

"I can hear your mind running around inside that gorgeous head of yours," Trey said sleepily.

Lane huffed and yanked the blanket up to cover his face. Gorgeous? Yeah right. Maybe Trey had suffered a head injury during the accident. It was the only way to explain his loss of sanity. He tried to still his thoughts, listening to Trey's breathing even out once more. Everything over the last two days seemed surreal. Nothing would have prepared him for this. Any of it. Happiness settled into his chest but it didn't last long. Memories of Gregory and the way he'd been ripped away from Lane stamped out any joy he might have been able to savor. Trey wouldn't be here long, and Lane didn't want to ever experience the pain of losing someone again.

After he turned eighteen, Lane had sought out Greg, hoping to be with him, but it hadn't gone the way he'd anticipated. He remembered the hatred on Greg's face when he answered the door and saw Lane. Gregory blamed him for being ousted from the one foster home he loved and being forced to move from place to place. Lane could only stand there and listen to the screaming and the obscenities Gregory threw at him while enduring the shoving as his back hit the wall and the spittle raining down onto his cheeks. The one dream Lane had held on to over the two years since their last time together shattered that day. Unable to bear it any longer, Lane turned and ran, his eyes burning and his heart aching beyond anything he'd experienced since his parents' death.

Later, once he gathered his emotions and dragged his body to the run-down, shoddy motel room he rented for one night, he made a plan to keep moving, to never stay in one place too long. He'd kept that promise to himself until Christmas Valley. The longer he stayed, the harder it got to find the urge to leave. He enjoyed his job, cared for Tal, and now had Chloe to think of. He reached down and petted

Chloe, scratching her behind her ears. Now Trey had disturbed the peace he'd felt since arriving here. He made Lane feel things he hadn't felt in a long time, but he couldn't open himself to that kind of hurt again. Ever. Trey didn't want a forever with him. After all, he'd be leaving again soon.

Exhaustion set in from the countless memories and thoughts chasing one another around in his mind, and Lane found it difficult to keep his eyes open. He tried to move away from Trey, but Trey had an unbreakable hold on him. Lane gave up fighting eventually and let go, falling into a restless sleep broken by haunting dreams.

WHEN LANE surfaced the next morning, it took him several long minutes to remember why he was shoved up against a hard form and why he could hear the steady thud of a beating heart. Once it came back to him he almost jolted upright, but the muscular arm around his waist kept him in place.

"Not yet" came a husky voice.

Lane swallowed a squeak and held himself stiff along the long length of Trey's body. "W-we should get up," he managed.

Trey issued a small moan and stretched, not releasing his hold on Lane. "It's still too early."

Horror set in when Lane felt his body responding to Trey and he began to harden. He tried to twist his body enough that it wouldn't be pressing into Trey, but Trey prevented him, nuzzling at his temple. Lane attempted to remind himself of his promise last night. It didn't work. A shudder rippled through him as Trey rocked his thigh against him.

"Stop." He dredged up a whisper.

Trey did as he asked, releasing him to scurry out from beneath the blankets, with a loud protest from Chloe, and into the biting cold of his apartment. Lane rushed into the bathroom and slammed the door closed, locking it. He leaned his back on the chilly wood and prayed for his arousal to go away. Shivers wracked his body, but he had no idea if they were from the freezing cold or from the desire raging through him. Lane couldn't remember feeling anything close to this way with Gregory. While Gregory's touches had made Lane feel good, none of them had caused his blood to sing out or his heart to race as though he were having a heart attack. Even the idea of Trey's mouth on his privates had him biting back a moan.

Lane moved over to the shower, wrenching it on, and stripped off his sweats and T-shirt. He stepped under the ice-cold spray and stayed there, shivering, until his hard-on had gone down. Once he'd calmed enough to think rationally, he added the hot water, sighing when it hit his skin, grateful to whoever had built the place for at least installing a propane water heater rather than an electric one. The bathroom steamed up immediately, fogging the mirror and dampening the floor. He didn't linger after that, shampooing his hair, washing his body, then turning off the water. He heard a knock at the door.

"Lane?"

He closed his eyes and held on to the faucets to keep his knees from going out. "Yeah?" he croaked.

"The storm let up. I'm going to go outside and see how bad the roads are. See if we can at least walk to my parents' place."

"Okay."

Lane heard silence and figured it meant Trey had left. He stepped out of the tub and snatched up a towel.

"Lane?" Trey surprised him.

He approached the closed door and rested one hand on the cold wood. He didn't answer, just waited.

"I'm sorry," Trey said.

Leaning forward, he rested his forehead against the door. He heard Trey leave the apartment. Every instinct in him screamed for him to run, to leave Christmas Valley, but he fought it. Trey wouldn't be around forever. He could handle a few days. Right?

By the time he grabbed clothing from his closet, dressed, and returned to the living area, Trey had returned. He stood inside the front door when Lane exited the bathroom the second time around. Snow covered his jeans up to his lower thighs and ice clung to the strands of his hair, sparkling in the early daylight. Lane swallowed hard. He couldn't lie to himself. The next few days were going to be hell.

Trey took off his jacket and hung it on the hook. "Sorry about the snow," he apologized.

Lane shrugged. "It'll dry."

Trey stomped off as much as he could from his jeans and boots onto the doormat. "It's going to be rough, but I think we can make it. I'd layer up with a couple of sweaters as well."

Lane went to the closet and took out a hoodie and another long-sleeve shirt.

"Those all you have?" Trey asked, frowning.

Nodding, Lane set them on the bed. "I've never had to worry about it before."

"It'll have to do. Make sure to wear at least two pairs of socks."

Lane moved to the kitchenette and silently started making coffee. Thankfully he had a gas stove instead of an electric stove. He filled a pot with water from the sink and set it on the burner. He lit the range and stood there, waiting for it to boil. An actual brewed mug of coffee would have been preferable, but without electricity, it wasn't an option.

His spine stiffened and shoulders tensed when Trey came closer and leaned against the counter.

"I really am sorry, Lane," Trey said softly. "I didn't mean to push you for anything."

Biting his lip, Lane stared at the water. "I can't," he said quietly.

"Can't what?" Trey asked.

"Y-you're leaving soon," Lane replied, dancing around the question.

"I know. This morning… it was a lack of common sense. When I felt you against me, I lost my head. I'm sorry."

Lane gave a jerky shake of his head. "It's okay."

"We should head out as soon as possible. It's going to be a long day."

"Do I have time for a cup of coffee?" Lane asked.

Trey chuckled. "Of course. Will you pour me one while I use your bathroom?"

"Yeah."

Lane listened as Trey went into the restroom and closed the door. He sagged into the counter and bowed his head. He didn't know if he was disappointed or relieved Trey wasn't going to act on his attraction to him. Then he yelled at himself mentally. What the hell was wrong with him? He wasn't stupid. He knew Trey wouldn't stay in Christmas Valley and Lane didn't want to leave. That didn't even factor in how much it would hurt being left behind again.

CHAPTER 4

W HEN HE heard the toilet flush, Lane shook himself from his thoughts and took out two mugs, set them on the counter, and spooned the crystallized coffee into them. Once the water boiled, he poured some into each and then added sugar and powdered creamer to his coffee, stirring with a spoon from the drawer. Trey joined him a few moments later, picked up the other mug, and took a sip.

"You make good coffee, Lane," Trey praised.

Lane wrinkled his nose. "It's instant. Besides, I don't know how anyone drinks it black."

"You gotta be hardcore for that," Trey bragged, winking.

A smile raised the corner of Lane's mouth and he shook his head. "I can't cook anything, but I have some Pop-Tarts if you want something to eat."

"It's probably a good idea if we both have something. I'm hoping we can make it to my parents' place in a couple of hours."

Lane retrieved the box from on top of the fridge, opening it and taking out two packages. He handed one to Trey and ripped the packaging on his own. "If the snow is that high up on you, it's going to be a lot more on me," Lane observed around a bite.

"I'm going to carry you."

A piece of tart went down wrong and Lane started choking, taking a sip of his coffee to soothe the fragment on its way. "I'm sorry?" Lane asked, uncertain he'd heard Trey correctly.

"I'm going to be brutally honest with you, Lane. Certain areas are going to be deeper than my knees, and I'm not even sure if we won't have to turn back rather quickly depending on how bad it is the farther away we get from here. The only reason I'm even taking the chance is because my parents will have the provisions to get through the next couple of days without freezing to death. We don't even know if there isn't another storm on the heels of this one, which could dump even more snow on us."

Fear dug its claws into Lane and his hand holding his Pop-Tart shook, the wrapper crinkling in the silence of the apartment. He could feel the blood leaving his cheeks and he set down his coffee mug, some of it sloshing over the side onto the counter. "Is—is it really that bad?"

"I'm not trying to scare you, but I need you to understand just how rough it could get if we don't at least try. The sooner we get to my parents' house, the better. Understand?"

Lane nodded. His appetite fled. He dropped the remainder of the pastry into the garbage can under the sink. Trey finished his last bite and tossed the empty wrapper in behind Lane's.

"Put on the rest of your clothing. Use a couple pairs of socks for your hands if you can. I'm going to need my gloves for the trip. Grab whatever you can't survive without for the next few days, and then we'll head out."

The only thing Lane cared about was Chloe. After he

emptied the rest of the pot of water down the sink and did as instructed, ignoring the comment about things he couldn't survive without since he didn't have much to begin with, and zipped up his hoodie, placing Chloe carefully inside, he put on his jacket. "I'm ready," Lane murmured, cradling his cat close.

"Let's do this!" Trey said enthusiastically, yanking on his gloves. "Lock the door behind us and follow me down the stairs."

When Lane stepped outside behind Trey, his lungs dragged in the crisp, cold air, instantly chilling him from the inside out. His gaze zeroed in on how deep the snow appeared. He could see where Trey had already gone several feet out from the bottom step and the path he'd forged through the white powder. The snow had risen up to just about cover the fourth step. Chloe moved inside his hoodie and Lane patted her through his jackets. He trailed after Trey until Trey reached the bottom.

Trey stooped over slightly. "Hop on."

Lane hesitated.

Trey glanced back over his shoulder. "Come on, Lane. I won't drop you if you're worried about that. I carry a lot of people around. Never dropped one yet," he promised.

Taking a breath, Lane placed his hands on Trey's shoulders, his feet already ankle deep in the snow on the fourth step, and he tried to keep from squishing Chloe as he placed himself against Trey's back. Trey wrapped his arms around the back of Lane's knees and hefted him up. To keep his balance, Lane was forced to slide his arms fully around Trey's neck.

"Relax and enjoy the ride," Trey said and started trudging forward through the snow.

Lane couldn't help holding his breath for the first several feet, but let it out on a small release when there didn't appear to be any hidden traps. Trey didn't even seem out of breath by the time they made it a few yards from his apartment steps. He glanced over to see his landlady staring at them out of the window and tossed her a wave.

She gave him a concerned look and opened the window enough to shout, "Are you boys okay?"

"Everything is fine, Mrs. Johnson," Lane called back. "How are you doing?"

"I'm perfectly well. Thank you for asking, Lane. Why don't you two come on in here and stay with me until the power is back on?"

Trey stopped and looked over at her. "Hey, Mrs. Johnson. We may take you up on that if we can't get to my parents' place."

"That's a long way to go," she protested. "You really don't need to."

"I'd prefer to try for my parents' place. I want to make sure they're okay and they may need my help clearing the snow. I think we'll be all right, but thank you," Trey replied.

Mrs. Johnson gave a skeptical look but didn't argue further. "You be careful out there, Trey Jenkins. Take care of Lane."

"I will, Mrs. Johnson. Thank you."

"Merry Christmas, you two."

"Merry Christmas, Mrs. Johnson," Lane returned. He'd actually forgotten it was Christmas. People everywhere would be opening their presents this morning, but with a little less cheer, he thought, wondering what the next couple of days would bring. Oh, the kids wouldn't think anything different, they just wanted whatever amazing toys Santa had brought them, but the parents could feel the difference.

Mrs. Johnson closed the window but continued to watch their progress, worry etched on her age-lined features.

"Are you sure we'll be able to get there?" Lane asked Trey. "Maybe we should stay with Mrs. Johnson."

"Yep. No problem. The house is just over on Vixen."

"That's far!" Lane exclaimed.

"Nah, not really. I've made the trip there many times."

Lane shivered as snow made its way down into his boots, dampening his socks. Trey continued to trudge forward, burrowing through the snow. It took at least fifteen to twenty minutes to make it to where Tal's truck was. Lane couldn't stop the gasp he let out when he saw the truck, white up to about the middle of the doors.

Trey sighed. "Tal really is going to kill me. I hope he stayed at the restaurant last night. If he's at our parents', I'm not going to live to see the day after Christmas."

"That's not true!" Lane exclaimed. "He wouldn't really do anything to you."

"He may."

Lane frowned. "Why are you so sure?"

"Because I wrecked his last truck too."

The wry tone Trey carried didn't escape Lane. "How?"

Trey's voice grew breathy as he talked while fighting his way through the knee-deep snow. "It was a few years back. I came home from college to visit, hooked up with some of my old friends, and I took his keys without asking. We got drunk and I ended up putting it in a tree."

Lane gave a horrified noise.

"I was a stupid kid. I ended up in jail for thirty days and Tal made me help him pay for the next one, even from college. Needless to say, I learned my lesson. Almost failed my classes that semester, having to miss them for thirty days. Took me a long time to find a fire department who'd give me a chance with a DUI on my record. That's why I ended up in Dallas."

Trey had started really puffing by the time they reached

the end of Lane's street. "Do you need to take a break?" Lane asked.

Shaking his head, Trey replied, "I want to get there as soon as we can. Like I said, sometimes these bad ones have another right on their tail. The sun's out, which is going to cause the snow to start to melt slightly and harden, making it harder to get there."

"We should have stayed at my apartment," Lane murmured.

"If another comes through, that apartment is going to become like an icebox. You'll be lucky to stay warm enough. I can't believe someone would be so reckless as to build that place without insulation or a fireplace, for that matter. You need to move."

Lane shook his head. "I can't afford anything else."

"Before I go back to Dallas, we'll find you something else. I'm sure my parents know someone who will give you a break on the rent."

The idea of Trey taking care of him made him uncomfortable. He had been on his own for so long, even before he became a legal adult, and it felt strange to have someone care enough to want to help him like that. "I'm fine where I am."

Trey stopped moving. "Anyone ever tell you that you are the most stubborn person alive?"

Lane started. "I am not."

"Are too."

"Am no—" Lane cut himself off. "Are we doing the 'are too, am not' game?"

Trey chuckled. "Maybe, but you still are."

Lane laughed softly and wiggled a bit. Trey shifted him up a little higher on his back. Chloe made a sound of protest and Lane gave a shushing noise. He didn't need her spooked while there was almost four feet of snow on the ground. "I'm just not used to people doing things for me," Lane admitted quietly as Trey began forging forward again.

"Friends do things for each other, Lane."

Was that what they were? Friends? Lane knew he'd already told himself they couldn't be anything else, but hearing Trey say it made his belly burn with disappointment and his heart sink deep down into the fire inside. He had to get ahold of himself or he was going to get whiplash from the yo-yoing his mind did on the subject.

Trey turned left onto the main street and started trudging toward Vixen. There appeared to be very little activity from the neighborhood, and it seemed rather eerie to Lane since usually the town bustled pretty heavily during the day. Lane saw a few curtains move and some people watching out of their windows, much like Mrs. Johnson.

"Maybe you should let me walk on my own," Lane murmured, suddenly uncomfortable.

"No offense, Lane, but you aren't exactly built for this. You'd be worn out in ten minutes." Trey even sounded a little out of breath now.

"People are watching." Lane could hear the discomfort in his own voice.

"So?"

"I just...." He didn't really know how to voice the reason he cared. It didn't matter about his own reputation, but it did about Trey's and his family's. No one knew him, but they certainly would know Trey, since he'd grown up there. In the six months Lane had lived in Christmas Valley, he hadn't picked up on the sense that people were prejudiced, but he hadn't exactly seen anyone else openly vocal about being gay. Lane hadn't even told Tal his proclivities. A man carrying another man might get others talking.

Trey stopped. "Don't let what anyone else thinks affect

you, Lane. The only thoughts that matter are your own. You can't let others influence who you are."

Lane dug his fingers into the collar of Trey's jacket. He remained silent and listened to the crunch of snow as Trey began moving again. He knew Trey's words made sense, but he didn't know how to apply them to himself. Over the years there'd been many people telling him who he should be, who he was, and even those who made him feel bad for being him. Greg's words that day five years ago rang in his ears. He'd called Lane a terrible word and told him he brought nothing but trouble everywhere he went. If it weren't for him, Trey would have been at home, warm and safe instead of trudging through the snow carrying Lane and his cat. For a long time, Lane had tried to convince himself Gregory was wrong, thinking he just was angry at Lane, but now... now he knew Gregory was right. He did cause problems for people.

The sun had risen high in the sky by the time they made it to the end of Vixen Street. Lane hadn't said a word in the hour it took for Trey to make a path to the street, a trip that normally wouldn't have taken fifteen minutes. He'd just rested his cheek against Trey's back and listened to Trey's breathing, figuring it would be best to not say anything. He knew Trey had to be exhausted already, but Trey kept going. The snow had begun to harden further, making it even more difficult for Trey to get through. Lane berated himself for being so stupid as to agree to let Trey drive him home last night. He should have just walked like he'd intended.

When Trey turned onto Vixen, he stumbled and both of them ended up in the snow. Lane was too surprised to make a sound until he found himself on top of Trey, partially buried in the snow. "Trey!" Lane exclaimed and scrambled off of him, immediately swallowed by the snow up to his waist. Chloe let out a frightened meow and Lane slid his arm under her inside his hoodie, bouncing her lightly. "It's okay, Chloe."

Trey swore and rolled over. He lifted his right leg until he could reach his ankle, gingerly touching it. "I think I twisted my ankle."

Lane immediately felt guilty. "I'm so sorry," he cried. "It's my fault."

Trey swung steel-gray eyes his way, stern and commanding. "This is not your fault, Lane. I caught my foot on something."

"What are we going to do?" Lane asked uncertainly. "You can't carry me now."

"My parents' home is only about halfway down the street. I can still carry you. We'll be fine. Can you give me a hand up?"

Worry caused Lane to nibble at his bottom lip. "But—"

"Lane, I'm fine." Trey cut him off. "Please give me your hand."

Lane reached out and placed his hand in Trey's. Trey used him for a bit of leverage to get up. Lane didn't miss the wince Trey made as he attempted to put weight on his ankle. "See? You can't carry me," Lane protested.

"The ice will help numb it. Now get on," Trey instructed, bending slightly at the waist and waiting for Lane to obey.

"I can walk," Lane replied stubbornly and started forcing his way through the snow.

Trey caught his elbow. Lane stopped but didn't turn around. "If you get tired, you let me know."

"I'll be fine. Like you said, it's only halfway down the block, right?"

"Right."

Lane continued moving, glancing back every couple of minutes to see Trey hobbling behind him, his own body leaving a trail for Trey to follow. It didn't take long for Lane's energy to be sapped, but he forged ahead. He'd been through a lot more than this, and he wanted to do whatever he could to help Trey, since it was his fault they were in the situation they were. His limbs shook with the exertion it took to get through the snow.

Chloe had started moving around and Lane stopped for a couple of seconds to move her higher up inside his clothes. "We're almost there, baby girl."

He heard a swearword behind him and turned to see Trey a couple feet back, struggling. Despite the cold he started to sweat out of anxiety and guilt. He moved to Trey's side and slid his arm around Trey's waist.

"It's my turn to help you," he replied.

"You can't hold my weight and walk," Trey grunted.

"Watch me. I'm stronger than I look."

Trey gave him a dubious look but didn't protest further. They started walking together. Lane kept one arm under Chloe and the other around Trey's waist. He would help Trey get to his parents' place even if it killed him. Then when the snowplows came through and things were back to normal, he'd return home and consider his options.

"How much farther?" Lane puffed after they'd gotten about a quarter of the way down the street.

"Not far. It's blue, with white shutters and dark trim."

Lane almost collapsed with relief when they finally saw the aforementioned house. They made it to the steps and Trey hobbled up them as the front door opened. Lane saw Tal's mother, whom he'd met a few times at the restaurant. "Trey! Lane! Lord Almighty, what in blazes are you two doing out here? Ed! We need some help here!"

"Merry Christmas, Ma," Trey joked without humor.

"What the heck were you two thinking?" she demanded as she came forward to the other side of Trey.

A man, almost the spitting image of Tal and Trey, exited

the front and rushed forward to relieve Trey from Lane and help him the rest of the way. "Where did you two come from?"

"We walked here, sir," Lane replied as he sagged against the railing, his arms and legs feeling like cooked noodles.

"Walked?" Mrs. Jenkins gasped.

Trey sighed. "It's a long story. One I'd rather tell inside. Did Tal make it here last night?"

"No. He called just before the phones went out to say he was staying at the restaurant with you. I'm guessing something came up." She gave a pointed look at Lane.

Lane flushed and looked at the floor as he followed them into the house. He didn't blame her for thinking it was his fault. After all, it was. Trey's father brought Trey over to the sofa by the fireplace and his mother went into action, tugging off his jacket and then working on his boots, easing off the one on his bad ankle. Trey hissed but didn't say anything. She gingerly removed his sock and looked at it. Lane winced when he saw the swelling.

Mrs. Jenkins poked and prodded, causing Trey to growl at her. "Don't fuss at me, young man. No one told you to do a fool thing like walk all the way here in four feet of snow."

"We had no choice, Ma."

"Let me get some bandages to wrap it up along with an ice pack and you can tell me all about it." Mrs. Jenkins stood.

"Can I help?" Lane asked.

"You stay here with my son and keep him company while I go get those things. Don't let him go anywhere. He hates when he needs doctoring."

Lane nodded and kneeled on the floor near the couch. Both of Trey's parents disappeared and Lane carefully undid his jacket and hoodie, removing Chloe and holding on to her so she didn't dart off. "Your mom blames me."

"What? No, she doesn't. She'd never think that."

"I saw it on her face."

Trey reached out and tucked a strand of Lane's hair behind his ear. "Lane, you have got to stop assuming things. My mom wouldn't ever believe that. She thinks we're together."

Confusion shot through Lane. He tilted his head to the side. "But we are together."

Laughter rumbled from Trey's chest. "Not like she means."

Realization set in and Lane's eyes widened while heat flooded his cheeks. "Oh."

"Yeah. Oh," Trey replied, laughter buried in his voice.

He felt stupid. He'd never been able to pick up on the subtleties some people chose to speak with. If his hands were free, he would have covered his face in embarrassment.

"Here we are," Mrs. Jenkins said as she returned carrying bandages and an ice pack wrapped in a hand towel. "Oh, who is this adorable little thing?" she asked when she spotted his cat.

"Chloe."

"You had her with you this whole way? Well, of course you did. You couldn't leave her on her own."

"No, ma'am."

"Pooh on this ma'am thing. Call me Ellen."

"Yes, ma—uh—Ellen."

"Good. Now let's get my fool son's ankle wrapped up while you two tell me what happened to cause you to end up on my front porch this afternoon."

While she carefully worked on his ankle, Trey relayed most of what had happened the previous evening, down to him tripping over something in the snow. Lane noticed he left out anything related to the two of them sharing a bed or the intimate moments first thing that morning. She kept glancing between them but didn't ask any questions. Once she'd finished with the bandage, she placed the ice pack on his ankle. Trey winced but didn't complain. Mrs. Jenkins stood, patting Trey's knee.

"Well, it's a good thing you ended up staying at his place overnight, Trey. Lane and Chloe may well have frozen to death if you hadn't been there. Your father was listening to the radio this morning, and they're saying there's another storm on its way in behind last night's."

"I'm glad I was there," Trey replied, yawning. "That apartment has atrocious insulation and no heating to speak of. I was telling Lane he needs to find another place. Thought maybe one of Dad's friends could help him out."

"I don't—" Lane tried to protest.

Trey pinned him in place with a hard stare. "You do need to move. Your place was almost as cold inside as it was outside this morning."

Lane bit his lip. "I still don't think I need to move," he muttered.

"That's a discussion for later, hmm? Now let's see if we have a nice saucer of milk for Miss Chloe there and perhaps a little bit of something for the both of you." Mrs. Jenkins interrupted their conversation.

"Thank you," Lane murmured, standing.

"May I hold her?" she asked.

"Of course." Lane handed Chloe to her and watched as she loved up on his cat, scratching Chloe under the chin and behind her ears. Chloe purred up a storm and snuggled into Mrs. Jenkins. "She likes you."

"I've always been a cat person, truthfully. I used to have several, but over the years, they've slowly died off. I didn't have the heart to raise any more. It's too painful to lose a family member." She laughed as Chloe butted her head against her chin. "You're a beautiful one, aren't you, sweetie?"

Chloe meowed and Lane smiled. "I found her right after I moved here."

"Well, let's go into the kitchen. I'll make everyone something to eat. Lane, honey, if you'd like to remove your jackets, there's a stand by the door. Just place them on it."

"Okay." Lane complied, taking off the jacket and hoodie, but left on the long-sleeved shirt over his T-shirt. He placed the two on the coat rack and followed her to the kitchen.

Mrs. Jenkins set Chloe on the counter and opened the fridge, taking out a small carton of milk. "If the power doesn't come back on soon, we're going to have to move some of this stuff outside into the snow. It's the only way to keep it from spoiling."

She took out a small saucer meant for a teacup and set it on the counter in front of Chloe, pouring some of the milk into the dish. Chloe sniffed at the bowl, took a tentative lick, and then started lapping it up. Lane petted her as she drank. "Thank you for being so kind."

"Nothing to it, sweetie. Would you mind handing me that loaf of bread out of the box there on the counter?"

Lane opened the wooden cabinet she'd indicated and took out the bread, passing it over to her. While she started making sandwiches for everyone, Lane took the chance to look around Trey and Tal's childhood home. Envy set in along with happiness for both of them. An island counter with light beige-colored marble and dark oak cabinets underneath sat in the center of a beautiful well-lit kitchen, windows lining three of the four walls. Stainless-steel appliances reminded him of Trey's eyes, sending a sliver of awareness through him at the thought of how they would change from steel to liquid silver depending on his mood or emotions. A matching dining table stood off to one side with four chairs and a pot of pretty yellow flowers in the middle.

Pictures cascaded over the walls, and Lane couldn't help

wandering up to them, hungry for any images of Trey as a child. His heart leapt into his throat when he caught sight of Trey as a teenager. Even back then, he'd been gorgeous. There were several of Trey with Tal and others with both of them and their parents. He saw one of Trey standing with another guy, both in tuxedos.

"That was his high school prom picture," Mrs. Jenkins said.

Lane turned to look at her and smiled slightly. "He took another guy?"

"Trey never kept his orientation a secret. When he first came out when he turned sixteen, we were worried. The concept of 'small towns, small minds' kept us awake quite a few nights, but no one seemed to care. Maybe because Trey was on the football team or maybe because he was quite built for his age. Either way we were thankful for everyone accepting him and not judging him. The horrors I've seen on the Internet and the news shock me every day. Children are thrown out of their homes by their own parents. I wouldn't call that a parent. A mother and father should love their child regardless of who they are."

He didn't respond, just returned to looking over the pictures. He had no idea if his own parents would have been okay with his orientation. They had died before he truly understood why girls never interested him like they had others. The boys in the locker room drew his gaze more than the scantily clad girls walking the halls of his high school.

Gregory taught him everything about being gay. Lane could still remember how Gregory called him out about staring at him while he dressed in their shared room. His heart beating hard at being caught, he confessed he had and apologized, staring at his lap where he sat on his bed. That was the first time Gregory kissed him, touched him. He learned what a blowjob was, coming way too quickly in

Gregory's mouth. The first time he felt the hard length of Gregory's shaft, Lane knew he'd never be interested in anything except the hot, pulsating flesh he held. Two days later Lane lost his virginity to Gregory. The memory made him wonder what Trey would feel like inside him.

A flush heated Lane's cheeks as he realized where his mind had gone and how his penis had thickened a bit at the idea. What horrified him was that he stood in the same kitchen with Trey's mother and had those thoughts! He cleared his throat and faced her. "Do you… uh… need any help?"

"That would be great. Would you mind grabbing the pitcher of tea out of the refrigerator, dear?"

Lane rushed to do as she bid, opening the door and taking out the container. He shut the fridge and placed the tea on the counter.

"There's some glasses in the cabinet next to the sink. Would you be a doll and grab four, please?" Mrs. Jenkins asked, slathering a slice of bread with mayonnaise. "You've worked for Tal for some time, haven't you, Lane?"

"Yes, ma'am."

"Now what did I tell you about this 'ma'am' stuff?"

"Ellen."

She gave a smile of satisfaction. "How long did you say that was?"

"Six months." Lane located the glasses and took out four, setting them carefully on the counter.

"Has Tal treated you well?"

"Oh yes," Lane replied. "He's helped me more than I can ever repay."

"My sons are very caring when it comes to someone who is in need. Tal has been through a lot with drifters needing a job when they come through here."

Lane could hear the strength behind her tone and knew

she sought reassurance as Trey had only two days ago. "I would never hurt him," he said quietly. "He's been kinder to me than anyone I've ever met."

Mrs. Jenkins gave a nod and smiled. "Good. Now pour us some glasses there and let's take this in to Trey, shall we?"

Lane poured the teas and set them on the serving tray Mrs. Jenkins pointed to. When she went to lift it, he stopped her and picked it up, following her into the living area once she picked up Chloe to bring with them. Trey had sprawled out on the couch and they could both see he'd fallen asleep, most likely exhausted from trekking through the snow with Lane on his back. Lane didn't want to wake him.

"Maybe we should eat in the kitchen," he murmured.

"My boys sleep like rocks. He wouldn't even hear a marching band if they came through here."

He gave Trey's mother a skeptical look but set the tray down on the coffee table.

"I'm going to go grab Ed. I'll be right back. Go ahead and start eating, sweetie."

Mrs. Jenkins set Chloe down on the floor and left the room to go find her husband. Lane sat down with his back against the couch close to Trey's side, ignoring his inner voice telling him to move away. He wanted to be near Trey as long as he could. Trey made him feel good inside, like everything would be okay. It was stupid to place that kind of emotion on someone who'd be gone in a few days, but he wanted to be selfish, even if only for a short time. He looked up at Trey and studied the strong cheekbones and firm lips. His gaze traced the ridge of Trey's brow and along the hard lines of his jaw, memorizing and embedding his features into his brain. He buried them away for the future when he wanted to remember.

Trey's eyelashes twitched and then slowly lifted,

surprising Lane, and he jerked his head around to stare at the tray of sandwiches.

"I told you I can't sleep when you're looking at me," Trey rasped.

Lane jumped when he felt Trey's hand on the back of his neck.

"I can feel you watching me," Trey murmured, massaging Lane's nape.

Pleasure surged through Lane and he tilted his head forward, a sigh escaping at the gentle pressure. Lane heard Trey move behind him until a breath whispered over Lane's ear.

The husky timbre of his voice sent chills down Lane's spine, but the words Trey said next obliterated him. "Do you have any idea how sexy and beautiful you are?"

CHAPTER 5

"I'M NOT," Lane breathed in disbelief after a moment of stunned silence.

"Yes, you are."

Lane went to shake his head in denial, but Trey stopped him by pressing his lips to the side of Lane's throat. A gasp bubbled up and Lane couldn't stop it from exploding outward, sounding loud in the quiet of the living room. Trey made a noise in the back of his throat and kissed him again, mouth wet and hot along the corded muscle beneath Lane's skin.

"We-we shou-shouldn't be—" Lane tried to stammer, but Trey didn't let him finish. He had removed his hand from the back of Lane's neck to grip Lane's chin, tipping his head toward Trey and covering Lane's mouth with his own. Everything else drifted away: his fear, the knowledge Trey would be leaving, that they were in Trey's parents' house and his parents could return any minute. None of it mattered. Nothing except the taste of Trey's kiss mattered. Lane opened beneath Trey's probing tongue, his mind cloudy and his common sense out the window.

The delicate sound of a throat clearing had Lane ripping his mouth from Trey's and blushing as red as a tomato. Oh God, what had he done? He couldn't look at either one of them, instead staring down at his lap in utter embarrassment.

"Hey, Ma. Where's Dad?"

"He was tinkering in the garage as usual. He'll be in a little later." She didn't say anything about what she'd interrupted, just handed one of the sandwiches and a glass of tea to Trey, who sat up as much as he could without putting his bad ankle off the pillow.

Lane couldn't imagine getting a single bite past the lump in his throat. He'd broken his promise to himself and now he *knew* what Trey's kiss tasted like. It would haunt him, drive him crazy in the middle of the night once he returned to his apartment, alone and lonely.

"Lane?"

He heard his name called and looked up.

"Eat something, dear. You're far too skinny."

Trey hummed in agreement behind him, his mouth full. Lane picked up his plate and fiddled with the sandwich. Trey nudged his shoulder gently. He set the dish back onto the coffee table. "May I use your restroom?" he asked without looking up.

"Of course, dear. You don't have to ask," Mrs. Jenkins admonished gently. "It's right down the hallway, first door on your right."

Lane stood and rushed out of the living room. He needed a few minutes to himself. Everything that had happened over the last few days was beginning to overwhelm him. He closed the door behind him and leaned against it for a moment, taking a few deep breaths and letting them out slow and even. Once he'd calmed enough, he rolled up the sleeves of his shirt and turned on the water to splash several handfuls on his face. He looked into the mirror at his reflection, droplets dripping into the sink and onto his shirt. Swollen lips caused him to wince. God, what Trey's mother must be thinking right now.

He picked up the hand towel lying on the counter next to the sink and dabbed at his face, watching himself and seeing the brightness in his eyes. Even Gregory had never made him feel so… desirable. He knew Trey wanted him. There was no denying that, not after the last twenty-four hours, not after the lust in Trey's kiss. But he couldn't give his heart to another person who would only break it into bits all over again when he left.

Steeling himself, Lane folded the towel and placed it back next to the sink. He gave a nod at his reflection and opened the door, walking down the hallway. He halted when he got close as he heard Mrs. Jenkins and Trey talking.

"…careful, honey."

"I am, Ma. You don't have to worry about me."

"I'm more worried about Lane than you."

"What do you mean by that?" Trey demanded.

"He's fragile, Trey. I don't know about his past, but even the few times I saw him at Tal's, I could tell he's going to need someone strong in his life, someone who can help him heal from whatever the past has done to him."

"And I'm not that person?" Trey asked.

"Not if you plan on leaving, Trey. It's not fair to him or you. You're going back to Texas after the New Year, and then where does that leave him?"

The question was met with silence and Lane's heart clenched. Even Trey knew he couldn't offer more than a week. He quietly moved back toward the bathroom and shut the door with a little bit of noise, letting them know he was on his way back. He felt guilty for eavesdropping, but he'd been rooted to the spot by the truth in Mrs. Jenkins's words.

Only his conscience had unglued his feet and forced him to stop waiting for Trey's answer that he was fairly sure never came.

Trey looked up when he entered the living room, but Lane kept his gaze averted, fighting the heat threatening to rush to his cheeks. Instead of sitting near the couch this time, he grabbed his plate and plunked down on an ottoman in front of a chair. He hadn't really taken much time to peruse the room before now and used it as an excuse to not look at either Trey or Mrs. Jenkins while he ate.

The couch, a dark brown plush style, rested against one wall near the fireplace with an oak-and-glass coffee table in between the couch and the matching chair and ottoman Lane sat on. An overstuffed recliner was on his left, one he could see had been well loved, most likely by Mr. Jenkins. A cozy rug covered a portion of the hardwood floors in the living area, and in the corner by the window stood a six-foot Christmas tree with dozens of colorful ornaments, a beautiful glittering star on top, and presents lining the skirt beneath it. He spotted several handmade ornaments that could only have been made by a child and wondered if they were Trey's.

The walls—three were a warm beige while the third was a darker honey color—were also lined with assorted photographs. It seemed Mrs. Jenkins loved photos of her family. There were lacy off-white curtains over the windows and a small faux tree with a wicker basket around the base near the door leading into the front entryway.

Sandwich finished, Lane stood and started cleaning up the dishes, placing them on the serving tray.

"You don't have to do that," Mrs. Jenkins insisted.

"It's the least I can do to thank you for your hospitality for me and Chloe."

Chloe meowed from where she lay playing with a loose

string in the area rug. Lane took the tray into the kitchen and set it on the counter. He turned on the faucet and started washing the dishes, setting them in the drain as he finished each one, surprised when the water actually started to heat. They must have a propane water heater in the house like he had in his apartment. It felt good to have something mindless to do for a change.

Mrs. Jenkins came in while he was drying the dishes and picked up the one plate he hadn't washed, the one with the remaining sandwich. She took it through a door off the kitchen, which Lane assumed led into the garage where Mr. Jenkins was "tinkering," as she'd said earlier.

Once he finished Lane wandered back into the living room and sank down to his knees near Chloe. She came right up to him and pressed into the side of his leg and started purring. Lane stroked the fur along her back and up to the tip of her tail.

"Lane?" Trey said quietly.

He didn't look at Trey.

"Are you mad with me?" Trey asked.

Lane shook his head.

"Hurt?"

Again another shake.

"I broke my promise to you, and I'm sorry. I couldn't help myself. You were sitting there so close to me, allowing me to touch you, and I lost my head. Again."

He remained silent for a while, listening to the log popping in the fireplace. Finally he replied, "For the first time since my parents died, I feel as though this place, Christmas Valley, maybe could become my home. I don't want to have to leave."

"Why would you have to leave?" Trey asked.

"Because I don't want to cause trouble for your family or you."

"Trouble? What are you talking about?"

Lane shrugged.

"No. You can't say something like that and not explain."

How could he tell Trey without giving too much away? What if something bad happened to them because of him? Like Gregory. "It doesn't matter," he murmured.

Trey made a frustrated noise and sat up entirely, bringing his bad ankle down to the floor, the ice pack sliding off and hitting the floor with a muffled thump.

"You should leave it elevated," Lane protested. "Otherwise the swelling won't go down."

"Screw the swelling," Trey snapped. "I want you to talk to me."

Lane frowned and stood to grab the ice pack. He reached for it, only to have Trey grab his wrist and yank him down onto the couch with him. Lane made a sound of surprise and tried to pull away.

"What did you mean by causing trouble?" Trey demanded, refusing to release him.

"I didn't mean anything," Lane replied, giving up the struggle to get free.

Trey scowled. "I wish I could beat the shit out of whoever put these damned ideas into your head."

"No one did," Lane lied.

"Don't try to bullshit me, Lane. You aren't a very good liar."

Anxiety struck Lane and he tugged at his wrist again. "Let go."

"Talk to me, then."

Anger dug in right along with the anxiety. "It's none of your business!" Lane shouted.

Trey seemed taken aback by his reaction and it caused him to loosen his grip, allowing Lane the chance to pull free. Lane jumped up from the couch and moved to the window, wrapping his arms around his waist. He kept his back ramrod straight as he heard Trey shift; a floorboard creaked, and then he felt Trey's hand on his shoulder, making him tense even further.

"You're right," Trey murmured. "I want to help you and it frustrates me that you won't allow me to do so, but that doesn't give me the right to pry when you aren't willing to share. I'm sorry."

Lane's anger died out and all that was left behind was a deep sorrow, a sadness he'd known since his parents died. He didn't even know if he could trust Trey to tell the truth right then. His instincts warred within him. One part of him wanted nothing more than to throw himself in Trey's arms and the consequences be damned, while the other part of him kept yelling at him to run, run as far away as he could and don't look back. All that lay in the direction of Trey was pain and loneliness once he left. It would be hard enough to look at Tal without thinking about Trey every time.

"I don't need rescuing," Lane whispered.

"Maybe not, but you need a friend, Lane. I'd like to be that friend."

Could they be friends? After the kiss and those moments in his bed before? The weakness in him pushed him toward having someone to lean on for a change. He fought it but lost the battle. "Okay."

"Yes?" Trey asked.

"Yes," Lane replied, still staring out at the houses covered in snow. The sky had already become overcast once more, dark clouds threatening to dump even more ice down on them. Was it an omen of the mistake he'd just made?

Trey squeezed Lane's shoulder. "Thank you."

Lane furrowed his brow and looked at Trey. "For what?"

"For giving me a chance," Trey replied simply.

"Oh."

Trey reached up and ruffled Lane's hair. "Can a friend ask you for a favor?"

Lane waited.

"Would you help me back to the couch?"

He immediately moved closer to Trey and slid his arm around Trey's waist. Trey leaned on him a bit as he assisted Trey over to the sofa. "You shouldn't have gotten up in the first place," Lane admonished as he lifted Trey's leg and placed his foot on the pillow.

"It was worth it," Trey said, smiling.

Lane scoffed and bent down to pick up the ice pack, hiding the thrill that went through him. He placed it on Trey's ankle. "Do you need anything else?"

"I do, but it isn't something appropriate right now," Trey replied, eyes twinkling with mirth.

Eyes widening, Lane shook his head and returned to his place on the rug with Chloe. The light in the room had dimmed somewhat due to the early evening hour as well as the clouds cloaking the sunset. Only the fireplace provided enough to see by.

Trey's parents returned shortly thereafter. "Let's grab some of the blankets from upstairs for you boys," Mrs. Jenkins said. "Lane, would you mind helping me?"

"Sure, ma—uh—Ellen," Lane replied. She gave him a look. "Sorry," he mumbled.

Mr. Jenkins went to the fireplace to add another log and make sure it didn't go out. Lane patted Chloe on the head and stood. "Be right back, baby girl."

She meowed but didn't try to follow him. Lane trailed behind Mrs. Jenkins upstairs. He loved the gleaming wood railing and the runner secured to the steps leading to the upper part of the house. More photos were staggered along the wall as they went up and into a hallway with the same warm beige paint on the walls, also carpeted.

"You have a beautiful home, Ellen."

"Thank you." She beamed. "It's been a little empty since the boys moved out, but a mother can't expect them to stay forever. What kind of home did you grow up in?"

Lane tensed. "Not like this. Small but nice. My dad worked construction while my mom stayed home to take care of me."

She led him to a door a little way down and opened it to reveal a closet with shelving holding towels, blankets, and various linens. "Where are your parents now?" she asked as she started handing blankets to him.

Jaw tight, he replied, "Dead."

Mrs. Jenkins halted her movements and turned to him. "I'm so sorry, dear," she said with sympathy, reaching out to brush her hand along his cheek. "How did it happen?"

"Car accident," he replied stoically.

"How old were you?"

"Fifteen."

She made a sound of dismay and hugged him, squishing the three blankets he held in his arms between them.

"I'm okay," he rasped. "It was a long time ago."

Pulling back, she looked him in the eye. "Losing someone you love is never easy. I'm guessing you were in foster care after that?"

Lane gave a brief nod. They were reaching a subject he didn't want to talk about. His expression must have shown her something, because she didn't ask any more questions about it. She resumed placing blankets in his arms.

"Where did you live before coming to Christmas Valley?"

"Several places. Nowhere in particular."

"Well, I hope you intend on staying here, dear. It's a wonderful place to build a home for yourself."

"I like it here," he replied simply.

"Good," she said with a smile. "I think that's enough blankets. Let's grab a few pillows from the guest room and Trey's old room."

Lane followed her into the first room and halted, his breath catching. Trey's, he guessed by the various football trophies on one shelf near the windows. The bed, queen-sized, sat against the middle of one wall with a nightstand on either side. Several posters of varying athletes were on the light blue walls. Lane could imagine Trey in here, studying or hanging out with friends. It was a room he'd have loved to have had in any of the foster homes he was in.

Mrs. Jenkins picked up both pillows from Trey's bed and made her way back into the hallway. Lane reluctantly trailed behind, eyes still scouring the room for whatever he could discover about Trey. She closed the door behind him and motioned for him to come with her to the next room. Lane didn't say anything as they completed their task and started heading downstairs with their haul.

Trey would remain on the couch and Lane would sleep in the chair with the ottoman. Trey's parents had a fireplace in their bedroom and would sleep in their bed.

"We had a rather late lunch, but is anyone hungry?" Mrs. Jenkins asked after they'd gotten Trey comfortable with two pillows and three of the six blankets.

"I am," Mr. Jenkins replied.

"You're always hungry," she teased him.

That set off a back-and-forth that made Lane smile. He picked up Chloe and placed her on the ottoman. She curled up instantly and closed her eyes. Lane scratched her ears. "I can help you make something," he offered once the two of them had gotten to the end of their playful bickering.

"That would be great," Mrs. Jenkins said.

For the next half hour, Lane listened to Mrs. Jenkins rambling about her cats, and eventually they got on the subject of books. It excited Lane to be able to talk about his favorite thing in the world. He found out her top books almost mirrored his own and that she also adored the Harry Potter series. He did, however, give her a raised eyebrow when she mentioned *Fifty Shades of Grey* and how much she loved it. She blushed when he called her out on it.

"It wasn't that bad," she protested.

Lane snorted. "Are you kidding?"

She giggled like a schoolgirl and Lane shook his head. "I still don't get what people saw in that series, but to each his own," he mused.

"If you'd like, there's several bookshelves in our office at the end of the hallway," she offered.

Lane brightened. "Really?"

"Sure. I can finish this up. Why don't you go find a book to read? It's going to be a long evening."

"I'll look after I help you."

Lane finished chopping the tomato she'd handed him moments ago, set the pieces in a small bowl near him, and picked up the cucumber. Mrs. Jenkins had started preparing a salad. A light meal, he supposed, since they'd eaten a short while ago.

He glanced out the window and saw it had already started to snow again. He shivered at the idea of being back in his ice-cold apartment. He was glad Trey had been there. Who knew what would have become of him and Chloe if he hadn't. Maybe moving like Trey suggested would be a good idea. After the snow let up, he could return to his apartment and start looking.

"This isn't really what I would call Christmas dinner," Mrs. Jenkins said once she finished the salad and started dishing it from the larger bowl into smaller ones. "But we'll make the best of it, hmm?"

Lane didn't know how she could be so bright and cheery with the snowstorm having ruined their Christmas. Poor Tal was stuck at the restaurant and Trey lay in the living area with a sprained ankle. They would be spending the evening huddled up against another snowstorm.

"I'm not really all that hungry," Lane said when she went to fill a fourth bowl. "If it's all right, I'd like to go look at those books now."

"Of course, dear. Straight down the hall, last door. If you get lost, send a signal," she teased, winking at him.

Smiling a bit at her joke, Lane walked slowly out of the kitchen and into the hallway. He spotted the door she mentioned and headed toward it. When he entered the room, his mouth dropped open. The walls were lined with bookshelves, almost like a library. Lane wandered along the shelves, eyeing more than one book he'd love to read and several others that were some of his favorites. He almost bumped into the desk on one side because he couldn't tear his gaze away long enough to look where he was going. When he spotted a hardcover copy of *War and Peace*, he stopped and pulled it free from the others. He traced the delicate letters on the cover with his fingers and opened it, breathing in the scent of the pages, a smell he loved more than any other. He closed the book and hugged it to his chest.

He returned to the living room. Trey had raised himself into a sitting position, his ankle resting on a pillow on the coffee table. Mr. Jenkins sat in the recliner while Mrs. Jenkins had joined Trey on the couch. Lane chose to sit on the carpet near the fire for light to be able to read.

"*War and Peace*," Mrs. Jenkins said, "such a great book."

Lane agreed and opened the cover, beginning to read. He heard them talking around him but completely tuned out whatever the topic pertained to. Soon, he lay on his stomach, propping his chin on his hands as he continued to read. At one point Mr. Jenkins placed another log on the fire, causing Lane to jump, but he quickly got back into the epic story.

He didn't even notice when Trey's parents got up to go to bed or when the wind began to blow harder, snow battering the house and the world around them. It was only when he heard a chuckle that he looked up. Trey was watching him and he realized they were alone. A particularly hard gust rattled the windows and Lane looked to find he could barely see out of them.

"Do you realize that you've been reading for about three hours now and didn't even look up when my parents said good night?" Trey asked, eyes sparkling.

Embarrassment set in. "Sorry," he mumbled and sat up, closing the book.

He knew the story well enough to know what page he was on without having to locate a bookmark. He'd never dog-ear a classic like *War and Peace*.

"Don't apologize. It's adorable."

Heat rushed to Lane's cheeks. He didn't say anything, merely got up and placed the book on the coffee table. "I need to use the restroom," he muttered and rushed out of the room.

After he'd relieved himself, he returned to find Trey lying down, no blankets on him. "You should cover up," Lane said, frowning.

"I mentioned before, I run hot. I'll be fine."

Lane figured it wasn't really his problem and moved to the chair and ottoman. He toed off his boots but left his socks on. Chloe lay fast asleep curled up on the blankets and merely opened one eye when Lane picked her up. He lifted the blankets and slid between them, shifting until he found a comfortable position with the pillow under his head. He settled Chloe beside him and stared at the fireplace.

When he first met Trey, he'd never have guessed he'd end

up here in Trey and Tal's parents' house or alone once more with the man who'd scared the bejeezus out of him merely a few days ago. What surprised him more than anything, though, was he no longer felt extremely shy around Trey, not like every other person he'd ever met. He found himself able to look Trey in the eye faster than he had Tal. He didn't know whether to be proud of himself or scared of what that meant. Tingles rippled along his skin and the hair on the back of his neck stood up as he thought back to the kiss from just hours ago. Despite the desire he knew Trey held for him, he didn't trust Trey to want more than sex.

"Will you tell me about how you grew up?" Trey asked suddenly, disturbing him from his thoughts.

"Why?" Lane didn't really want to rehash that, especially with Trey.

"Because I'd like to know and because I already shared my childhood with you."

Trey had him there. He fingered the corner of his pillow, still watching the fire crackling in the hearth. "It wasn't anything special. Certainly nothing like yours," Lane finally murmured. "I grew up in a home smaller than this one and was a bit of what people consider nerdy. I preferred to read than to play outside."

"So you loved books even back then?"

"Yeah. My mom loved to read. She taught me to before I was four, and by the time I started school, I was able to read books meant for older kids." Lane's heart hurt at the memory of his mother. "It's the only thing I have left of her."

"You don't have any pictures of your parents?"

"After moving so many times after they died, anything I had got lost. I can barely remember what they even looked like," Lane admitted softly.

Trey made a soft sound in his throat. "I'm sorry."

"It was a long time ago," Lane said.

"Maybe so, but it still can't be easy. Tal mentioned you were in foster homes until you were eighteen?"

Lane tensed, his fingers clenching on the pillow. He'd shared that with Tal in confidence and felt hurt and angry that Tal had shared it so easily with Trey. "Yeah," he managed.

"How many were you in?"

"Six."

"Wow, that's a lot. You didn't find one you wanted to stay in?"

Lane wondered if Trey had any idea what it was like. You didn't get to choose. The people chose to keep you, and none of them were people who were interested in keeping any, let alone a fifteen-year-old boy. "No," he answered, not offering any further clarification.

"Why not? Did you not like any of them?"

He'd liked the one he was in with Gregory. They were the only ones who were good to the children they fostered, but after discovering him and Gregory, they changed, became hateful and cruel, immediately calling for Lane's removal. They blamed Lane for turning Gregory into something so shameful, since Gregory was there first and had never showed any signs of being *sick*.

"You don't get a choice," Lane finally informed Trey. "They're the ones who get to choose. No one wanted to keep me."

Trey didn't respond right away, the only sound the popping noise of the log settling. When he finally spoke, Lane's breath caught in surprise. "They were crazy not to."

Lane lifted the shoulder he wasn't leaning on in a shrug, but knew Trey couldn't see it. "I was too old."

"That's bullshit," Trey exclaimed. "You were fifteen. How could they think you were too old?"

"People want babies, not teenagers, especially ones they

believe are an abomination." Lane let it slip before he could stop the word.

"What did you just say?" Trey demanded.

Lane winced. He hadn't meant to say that out loud and was hoping Trey would let it go, but even with only knowing Trey for less than a week, he had a feeling Trey wouldn't miss it. "It's nothing," he mumbled.

"It's not nothing," Trey growled. "Who told you that you were an abomination? Why would they say something so hurtful?"

Lane wanted to slap himself. He hadn't wanted to open that can of worms. He searched for the words to respond.

"Lane?" Trey prodded.

He remained silent.

"Don't make me get up again," Trey threatened.

Sighing, Lane finally whispered, "They found out I was gay."

"I'm sorry, what?"

"They found out I was gay," Lane repeated, a little louder this time.

Sheer silence met his declaration and Lane wondered if Trey was going to say anything. When a full minute went with no response from Trey, Lane peeked in Trey's direction, only for his throat to close over. Rage dominated Trey's handsome features. He saw Trey swallow more than once, fighting back the emotion from what he could understand. Was Trey angry at him?

"You. Are. Not. An. Abomination," Trey finally ground out, his voice hoarse but hard.

Lane had carried those words with him for years and probably would for a long time. He'd never forget the way their foster father grabbed him out of Gregory's bed and threw him into the hallway, his back slamming into the wall, or the sound of the wife screaming as he hightailed it downstairs, struggling to cover himself with his hands.

He'd curled up in a ball on the floor between the couch and an entertainment center, waiting for a rain of fists. They never came, but his clothing did, and their foster father demanded he get dressed. They had already called the social worker; she'd be coming to get Lane in an hour, so he'd better get his stuff together.

Gregory wasn't in the room when he went upstairs to pack his few belongings. Their foster mother had taken Gregory into their room and shut the door. He wasn't even able to say good-bye before the social worker took him away. All he could remember were the tears and his heart breaking into pieces as she drove away.

"Did you hear me, Lane?" Trey grated.

"Yes," Lane managed, his voice a thread in the darkness between them.

"Loving another man does not make you an abomination. It doesn't make you anything except a human being who got the short end of the stick at a young age by being put in a home where anyone could think that of a child or another person, period. Never think of yourself that way ever again. You understand me?"

Lane made a noise but didn't say anything.

"God, there are some people in this world I could just beat the ever-living hell out of. Ignorance doesn't give them the right to put such thoughts in your head."

The windows rattled with another gust of wind and Lane couldn't help the small smile on his lips at Trey's outburst on his behalf. He buried his face in his pillow and tried to make it go away, but it didn't seem to want to. It only grew wider.

"Where else have you lived?" Trey asked, changing the subject.

"A few places," Lane replied vaguely.

"Anywhere specific?"

Lane figured Trey wouldn't let it go and named a couple of the more well-known places he'd put down stakes for a short time. "Carson City, Redding, and some small places you probably wouldn't have heard of."

"That's quite a jump. Were you heading anywhere specific or just moving around?"

A yawn broke free and Lane covered his mouth to stifle it. "Moving around."

"Ever get into Texas?"

"No."

"Where'd you grow up?"

"San Diego."

"California native, huh?"

Lane's eyelids drooped and he struggled to keep them open. "Uh-huh," he said on a yawn.

"Did you get to meet any celebrities living there?"

"Uh-uh," Lane grunted, seconds from drifting to sleep.

"Good night, Lane."

"G'night," Lane managed.

He heard Trey chuckle as he slipped into darkness and wondered if Trey was laughing at him.

CHAPTER 6

THE SOUND of voices brought him out of one of the best sleeps he'd had in a long time. He opened his eyes slowly, blinking at the light, to see Trey sitting up with his mother on the couch beside him. He didn't really want to move, too comfortable beneath the blankets, but he knew Chloe would be desperate to use the litter box, if she hadn't already tried to find somewhere hidden in the house, and he had no idea how to make that happen. His bladder also protested, demanding he get up. He conceded the fight and straightened in the chair.

"Oh, we didn't wake you, did we, dear?" Mrs. Jenkins asked, concerned.

He shook his head and stood, stretching with a yawn. When he realized Trey was watching him, he flushed and dropped his gaze. Lane mumbled a good morning and fled the room to use the bathroom. Horror brought him up short as he saw himself in the mirror. His hair stuck up in several places and he had those icky crusty things in the corners of his eyes. He groaned and savagely combed his fingers through his hair. No matter how much he would like to impress Trey, somehow he kept showing Trey the bad side of himself. Of course, maybe now it wouldn't be so hard for Trey to ignore him once he saw how Lane woke up in the mornings.

Sighing, he used the toilet, washed his hands and face, and squeezed out a little bit of the toothpaste sitting on the counter to finger brush his teeth.

After he made sure he no longer looked like something out of a horror movie, Lane exited and wandered back to the living area, his thoughts on how he'd find a makeshift litter box. Entering the living room, Lane halted and frowned when he saw Chloe wasn't where he'd left her. Aww crap. He prayed she didn't intend on peeing or pooping on the floor somewhere.

"Ma's got Chloe," Trey offered when he saw Lane's expression.

Relief swamped him. "Oh. Okay."

"She figured Chloe would need somewhere to go. She mentioned some of her old cat stuff was in the garage."

Lane stood there, uncertain on what he should be doing right then. He had anticipated Chloe taking up his attention, at least for a little bit, but now that Mrs. Jenkins had taken that off his hands, he didn't know how to keep his focus away from Trey.

"Come sit with me, Lane," Trey said.

"I should—"

Trey stopped him with a look and Lane shifted a bit, biting his bottom lip in uncertainty.

"You do that a lot."

Lane tilted his head to the side, not really understanding what Trey was talking about.

"Biting your lip," Trey explained, shadows darkening his eyes, and Lane suddenly felt extremely hot all over.

He shrugged.

"Will you please come sit?" Trey asked again.

Stomach twisting, Lane walked the few feet to the couch and sank down on the edge, back straight as an arrow. He let out a surprised noise when Trey gripped his arm and yanked him against his side in a half hug.

"Good morning," Trey said.

"G-good morning," Lane stuttered. That was when Lane realized Trey wasn't wearing the same clothes from last night. He remembered he didn't have any of his own clothing, not having thought to bring any, and prayed he didn't smell funny from having worn and slept in the same ones.

"Ma dug out some clothes she thinks might fit you from when I was younger," Trey said, seeming to have read his mind. He still hadn't released Lane.

"Oh. Thank you," Lane murmured, his mind jumping to the thought of wearing something that had been against Trey's own skin, even though it had been washed, most likely.

Trey hummed and said, "Ma doesn't really believe in throwing anything out. She's always said you never know when you're going to need it again. In this instance, I guess she was right. You're far too slender for anything I have now."

Lane read "slender" as a nice way to say "skimpy." He bit his bottom lip again, only to jump in surprise when Trey suddenly reached up and tugged it out from between his teeth. "Stop," Trey muttered.

"I-I'm sorry," Lane stammered.

Trey sighed and tipped his head back, rubbing at his eyes with his free hand. "Don't apologize."

"I'm so—"

Covering Lane's mouth with his hand, Trey looked at Lane. "You have no idea, do you?"

Lane didn't really understand, no. He nervously licked his

lips, accidentally tasting the salt on Trey's palm. Steel gray became liquid silver in a split second, but Trey closed his eyes before Lane could even begin to try and read Trey's expression. Trey dropped his hand from Lane's mouth and breathed in deep. Lane sensed Trey struggling with something and tilted his head to the side.

"Is something wrong?" Lane asked.

A derisive chuckle left Trey. "Nothing anyone can help me with," Trey replied, opening his eyes again.

"I sh-should go find your mom and Chloe," Lane murmured.

"That might be a good idea."

Lane fought against the burning desire to stay at Trey's side and stood. "I'll b-be right back."

He scurried out of the room and into the kitchen where he leaned against the counter, head bent and eyes closed. The feelings rushing over and through him confused him. He knew enough about sex to know his body wanted Trey, but his heart wouldn't stop screaming at him that the longer he was around Trey, the harder it would be when Trey left. It wasn't as if he had a choice right now, but he needed to stop allowing Trey to draw him in like that. All it would bring in the end was pain and loneliness.

When he heard the door leading to the garage close, he jerked his head up and tried to hide his emotions behind a smile at Mrs. Jenkins. "I'm sorry you had to do that."

Mrs. Jenkins regarded him for a moment, causing him to break out in a cold sweat. She didn't say anything, though, which sent relief rushing into his belly. "It's okay, dear. I don't mind. It actually reminded me of how much I miss my own fur babies."

"How many did you have?" Lane asked as he took Chloe from her.

"Four. I started out with one when I was in college, and

then when I got married to Ed, I found another one hiding in our garage. A friend of mine gave me one she couldn't keep because her soon-to-be husband was allergic, and the fourth one, well, she kind of just showed up in front of the house one day."

She smiled at him. "How did you happen to come across Ms. Chloe?"

Lane reiterated how he found her out behind the restaurant one day. "She was only a few months old. It took some time to gain her trust, but eventually she let me pet her and then pick her up. I took her home and have had her ever since."

"She is very sweet. Where did you come up with her name?" Mrs. Jenkins asked as she pulled out a gallon of milk from the fridge and set it on the counter. She frowned. "We're going to have to move this stuff to the outside today."

Lane hesitated but then replied, "It was my mom's name."

Mrs. Jenkins gave him a knowing look. "That is a beautiful name, sweetheart. I'm sure your mom would have loved it."

He nuzzled Chloe. "I hope so."

"She would have," Mrs. Jenkins insisted. "A mother knows these things."

Smiling, Lane said, "Thanks."

"Nothing to it, dear. Now would you be a doll and grab a bowl out of the third cabinet for me?"

Lane set Chloe on the floor and hurried to do as she asked, handing it to her. She filled it with some cereal and a bit of the milk before giving it to Lane. "Should I take this to Trey?" he asked.

"No, sweetie. That's for you. Trey already ate this morning."

"Oh," Lane said, stunned she had thought of him.

"You know where the silverware is. Grab a spoon and

have a seat. Keep me company while I get a box and start putting the most perishable stuff in it, hmm?"

"Okay," Lane murmured and took a spoon from the drawer. He pulled out a chair and sat down.

She disappeared for a minute back into the garage and returned with a cardboard box. He scooped up a mouthful of flakes and shoved them in his mouth, watching as she started loading the milk, eggs, and several other items into the box.

"I dug out some of Trey's stuff from when he was in high school. You may have to roll up the pant legs, Lane, but hopefully they'll fit you enough to where I can hand-wash your clothes and hang them to dry by the fireplace."

"You don't have to do that," Lane mumbled around a mouthful of cereal.

"Don't talk with food in your mouth," she admonished without heat. He flushed. "I don't have to do anything I don't want to do, dear, but you certainly can't walk around in those same clothes for the next few days. Ed said the plows probably won't be through for at least twenty-four hours. The power may be another couple of days after that. Trey can take you over to get some of your own stuff once the roads are cleared, but you're staying here until the power comes back."

"I don't want to put you out," Lane protested, dropping his spoon into the bowl.

"You aren't putting us out, and there is no way you are returning to that apartment without heat. I already spoke with Ed about finding you a new place, and he said Joe, his friend from the hardware store, has a place available over on Comet. He'll talk to Joe once everything is sorted."

Lane couldn't have felt more uncomfortable. "I don't think—"

She went on as though she hadn't heard him. "Joe is a good man too. He'll do right by you, and I am certain the place will have proper heating. Imagine. Building a place without a way to keep warm in a climate like ours!" She tsked a couple of times. "After breakfast I thought we could play a game or two to pass the time, hmm?"

Lane's head whirled with the abrupt changes in topics. "Sure," he mumbled, stabbing at his cereal. He truly didn't like the idea of anyone helping him. If his days hitchhiking had taught him anything at all, it was help came with strings, usually. Several of the men who'd given him a lift had asked for either money for gas or for Lane to do things that made him shudder at the thought.

"We have Monopoly," she interrupted. "Trey usually wins the game and never lets us hear the end of it."

A pang wrenched Lane's heart. His parents had instituted a game night every Friday since Lane turned five. Monopoly was his favorite. He clenched his fingers on his spoon.

Mrs. Jenkins sat in the chair across from him. "Have you ever played it before?"

He nodded. "A long time ago."

"We also have Scrabble, but Ed and Trey balk at playing it because I always win." She laughed lightly. "There's a few others in the closet, but those were the two we always ended up playing whenever Trey and Tal stuck around the house long enough as teenagers. After Trey joined the football team and discovered boys, he wasn't around as often. Tal was more into spending time with us than Trey. Since I can remember, Trey talked about nothing except getting out of Christmas Valley."

Lane could hear the sadness buried in her voice and felt bad for her. He reached out and placed his hand on top of hers. She smiled at him and squeezed his fingers in thanks for his comfort.

"Trey's always been more adventurous than Tal. From the minute he could walk, Trey did nothing except give me heart palpitations. I still remember the many scrapes and bruises I helped him through. I guess he hasn't changed much, considering his current profession. I kind of hoped he'd get it out of his system and eventually come home."

"Maybe he will someday?" Lane suggested.

Mrs. Jenkins smiled again, this time a lot sadder than before. "I don't think so, sweetheart. He's happy living in a big city. Christmas Valley could never hold his attention for long."

Lane read into her words and knew exactly what she was trying to gently tell him. His appetite fled and he pushed his bowl away. The cereal had gone soggy anyway. "I understand."

"Ed should be down shortly. I'll get this cleaned up if you'd like to read for a little bit."

He shook his head. He wasn't really in the mood to read. "That's okay. I can get the games from the closet if you tell me where they are."

She gave him directions on where to find them and he left to grab both games, reading through the others available. He also saw a deck of cards and took those too. Mrs. Jenkins had already gone into the living room when he finished. She'd chosen to sit with Trey, and Lane decided to sit on the floor in front of the coffee table. Mr. Jenkins popped in a minute later. Lane opened Monopoly, stilling his emotions about the game reminding him of his parents.

Trey sat forward and started helping him set everything up, claiming the car for himself. Lane chose the dog while Mrs. Jenkins took the iron and Mr. Jenkins the top hat. Lane remained quiet as the three of them ribbed and teased one another. He smiled a few times and spoke whenever he was addressed but didn't really participate in the taunting.

It came down to him and Trey about an hour later. Trey

had Boardwalk and Park Place while Lane had all four rail-roads and the purples and oranges. Trey's parents were waiting with bated breath to see if Trey could finally be beat. Lane rolled the dice and landed on Park Place, which nearly wiped out his bank, but then Trey landed on his property. It became an almost endless cycle, and for another hour, they went back and forth until finally, by the skin of his teeth, Lane beat Trey.

"Oh my goodness," Mrs. Jenkins breathed and sat back, her eyes wide.

Trey gave a sardonic smile and ran a hand through his hair. "Well… I can honestly say I didn't expect that."

Lane winced. "I'm so—"

"Don't say it," Trey growled without heat. "It was a good game. I lost fair and square."

"Finally," Mr. Jenkins goaded and Lane couldn't help feeling guilty.

"I'm sure I won't hear the end of it." Trey laughed and winked at Lane.

"Scrabble now!" Mrs. Jenkins demanded while Trey and Mr. Jenkins let out a groan.

They grumbled but complied, and the time passed quickly with the three of them still prodding one another, especially whenever one of them would take too long to answer. Lane had to hide a smile more than once. His chest felt warm and tight. He'd missed being part of a real family. Seeing the way they treated one another made his throat close over, and he had to swallow several times in order to answer whenever they spoke to him directly.

It was late in the afternoon by the time they had finished. Chloe had curled up beside Lane and was fast asleep. Lane helped Mrs. Jenkins clean up, leaving the cards for later. "I have some pretzels if you boys want some playing chips," Mrs. Jenkins offered.

Trey glanced at Lane, but answered, "Maybe later on, Ma. I think I need to raise my foot again for a bit."

Lane returned the games to the closet and came back to pick up the book he'd been reading. He curled up in the chair and propped the book on the arm. It didn't take long for him to lose himself in the story once more, and by the time his stomach let out a large gurgle reminding him he hadn't finished his breakfast or eaten lunch, he was squinting to see the words on the page.

"You should be more careful," Trey said quietly. "You're going to strain your eyes."

Setting the book back onto the coffee table, Lane stretched with a small moan as bones popped and muscles burned from being in the same position for a long time. He realized both Trey's parents were nowhere to be seen again. "I didn't even notice," he replied honestly.

Trey grunted. "Hopefully tomorrow I can get up and be mobile. I'm not much for sitting."

Lane nodded and glanced out the window. The sun had fallen behind the houses and he could just make out the last fingers of light slowly disappearing. "I hope Tal is all right," Lane murmured.

"There's a fireplace in the room upstairs, and don't forget the one in the main room."

"Right," Lane replied distractedly.

"The snowplows will probably come through tomorrow and then Tal will be able to get here. Although I'm not sure that's necessarily a good thing right now."

Lane frowned. "Why not?"

"I can't run, and Tal will know something happened to his truck."

"Oh."

"It's okay. I'll pay to get it fixed. He knows that."

"I should be the one!" Lane exclaimed. "It's my fault you took it in the first place."

Trey sighed. "Do we have to have this conversation again, Lane?"

"But if you hadn't taken me home—!"

"You would have frozen to death in that shitty excuse for an apartment!" Trey snapped. "I wasn't going to let you walk home that night. The truck doesn't matter. It's an object, something that can easily be replaced. You can't!"

Lane's jaw snapped shut with an audible click. He rubbed at his face with his hands and bit back the instinctive argument. He didn't want to go in circles and he didn't know how to handle someone actually caring about what happened to him. No one since his parents, anyway. And Tal, the voice in the back of his mind whispered. Lane stilled and realized he'd become comfortable with Tal's caring for him. Oh, he didn't let Tal do everything or accept it without protest, but he no longer felt it was wrong or that it came with strings. When had that happened?

Mrs. Jenkins stalled whatever else he may have said by appearing in the doorway with a tray loaded with two bowls of steaming-hot soup and two mugs of hot cocoa. Lane gave her a surprised look. "Ed located a couple of the Sterno burners in the garage so I could make something hot for us instead. I thought we could all keep Trey company while we eat this time."

Lane jumped up to take it from her and set it on the table. She handed off one of the mugs and a bowl to Trey and then set the other two on the table before picking up the tray. "Just gotta grab the other two for myself and Ed."

He started to follow her to help but she waved him back. "Have a seat. Eat it while it's hot."

He hesitated but moved to sit beside the coffee table, refusing to look up at Trey as he stirred and then blew on a spoonful. Mr. and Mrs. Jenkins joined them a moment later and Mrs. Jenkins started asking Lane about himself again. The questions were inane and just about what he liked to do. She seemed to understand he didn't want to discuss the foster homes or his past.

Lane slowly relaxed and started smiling as she told tales about Trey and Tal when they were younger. He listened with rapt attention, greedy to learn anything he could about Trey. He knew it made him a glutton for punishment, but somehow he couldn't turn off the part of him that wanted Trey. The kiss from the day before had only left him wanting more and knowing he couldn't have it, shouldn't have it. He didn't deserve anything after what happened with Gregory. The minute the power came back on, Lane would return to his apartment and bury his feelings as deep as he could manage.

"Every year we throw a New Year's Eve party," Mrs. Jenkins said, interrupting his thoughts. "I'd like you to come, Lane."

"Oh, I've already imposed enough," Lane protested.

"Please come," she urged. "It'll be fun, and since we didn't really get to have our usual Christmas, we have to make up for it. Please?"

Lane felt cornered. He wanted to avoid being around Trey as much as possible.

"Trey, talk him into it," Mrs. Jenkins demanded.

"Ma, if he doesn't want to come, don't force him."

Hiding a wince, Lane bit his lower lip and looked away. "I'll think about it," he lied, knowing he wouldn't.

She sighed but accepted his answer. "I really hope you'll come, dear."

Mr. Jenkins must have fallen asleep at some point because he let out a loud snore all of a sudden, disturbing the silence.

Lane stifled a nervous laugh and stood, beginning to clear up the mess from their dinner.

"You don't have to clean up."

"I want to, Ellen."

"You're such a good boy," she complimented, causing Lane to blush.

"Thank you," he mumbled as he picked up the tray and fled into the kitchen, which was lit only by a few candles Mrs. Jenkins had left burning.

He washed everything slowly, taking the time away to remind himself of what pain lay ahead if he continued to allow them to pull him in, only to lose them after the holidays. After all, it's not like they wanted him around forever. They'd been thrown together by circumstance, and once he went back home, they'd forget about him and go back to their lives.

With that in mind, he finished cleaning the dishes and drying them, leaving them stacked neatly on the counter, and went to use the restroom before returning to the living room. He didn't say anything, just curled up in the chair with Chloe on the ottoman and stared into the fire.

Depression swamped him, crashing over him and drowning him. His throat tightened and his eyes burned. What he wouldn't give to have a family of his own, to be a part of one as loving as Trey's, to be welcomed home with open arms and feel wanted. He dug his fingers into the arm of the chair, working hard to fight off the emotion. Being upset about it wouldn't change the reality of his life, and he didn't want to alert the others to his distress. They wouldn't let him be until he shared, and right now, he couldn't. He closed his eyes, hoping to find bliss in the comforting darkness of unconsciousness.

. . .

SLEEP MUST have overcome him at some point, because a muted bang woke him. He blinked open his eyes to see Trey standing and scowling, holding his knee. Lane sat up and rubbed at his eyes. "You okay?"

"I'm fine," Trey huffed and plopped down on the couch. "Danged table jumped out and bit me."

Lane huffed with husky laughter.

Trey gave him a mock glare. "Go ahead and laugh at my pain."

Schooling his features as much as he could, Lane replied, "I'm sorry. Is your knee all right?"

"Yeah, it's okay."

"Good." Lane yawned. "What were you doing?"

"Had to put another log on the fire."

Lane realized at that moment a blanket had been placed over him. He knew he'd fallen asleep uncovered. Had Trey done it? Maybe it was Trey's mother. "How is your ankle doing?"

"Better than expected. Don't think it was as bad as originally thought."

Closing his eyes, Lane made a sound of satisfaction. "That's great," he mumbled.

"Lane?"

"Hmm?" he breathed.

After a moment Trey said, "Never mind. Go to sleep."

Lane barely heard his reply.

THE NEXT morning the couch was empty and Lane sat up, stretching. He didn't think it was too late in the morning since there was still a hint of darkness in the house. He stood up off the chair, patted Chloe, who opened one eye and then closed it, and started toward the bathroom. He wondered if Mrs. Jenkins would mind if he used some of the hot water to take a quick shower.

He reached out to open the door, only to jump back in surprise when it swung open. Trey stood there completely naked from the waist up, a towel slung low around his hips and another around his neck. Droplets of water trickled down the tanned, smooth, muscular skin of Trey's chest. Not a single hair covered Trey's chest, only a spattering down his lower abs into his towel. Dark, dusty-rose nipples were beaded into stiff nubs from the cold. Lane's mouth dried out and he felt his penis swelling.

Trey must have seen the effect he had on Lane, because he stepped closer, forcing Lane the short distance to the wall behind him. "You shouldn't be looking at me like that," Trey growled softly.

Lane licked his lips, trying to find the words. A small groan tore free from Trey and suddenly Lane found himself drowning in Trey's kiss. He gasped, instinctively reaching up to grip Trey's broad shoulders. He couldn't prevent the mewling noise he gave when Trey shoved a hard thigh between his legs, pressing against him. Lane dug his fingers into Trey's muscles, struggling to breathe and feel anything beyond Trey.

"Lane," Trey husked, trailing his lips along Lane's jawline to his throat.

Lust spiraled tighter within Lane as Trey sucked at the skin between his shoulder and neck, hot and wet and oh so obliterating. The towel around Trey's waist loosened and fell, puddling around his feet. Lane felt Trey's stiff length digging into his abdomen and whimpered.

"God, you taste so good," Trey rumbled near his ear, tracing the delicate outer shell with his tongue, sending a ripple of quivers through Lane.

"Trey," Lane begged, not even knowing what he wanted.

"I love the sound of my name on your lips," Trey sighed before capturing said body part once more.

Desire stuffed Lane's head with cotton and the only thing he could do was blindly accept the passion from Trey. Nothing he'd ever experienced in his life could compare to what ripped through him right then. Not even with Gregory.

The thought of Gregory reminded him of the horrible mistake he was making, a bucket of cold water thrown over his heated skin. He tore his mouth from Trey's.

"No," he croaked.

Trey didn't appear to hear him or chose not to when he continued to lick and nip along Lane's jaw and throat and rocked his thigh against Lane's groin.

"Stop," Lane demanded, shoving at Trey's chest.

The movement and the coldness in Lane's voice must have brought Trey to his senses. He released Lane and stepped back, breathing heavy, body flushed and member straining with lust. Lane averted his eyes from the sight and clenched his teeth.

Trey moved slowly, picking up his towel and wrapping it around his waist. "Lane, I—"

"Please don't touch me again," Lane interrupted, still not looking at Trey.

Trey swore under his breath. "I didn't mean—"

Lane didn't let him finish. He brushed past Trey and into the bathroom, shutting the door with a soft snick. He heard Trey swear again through the wood and sank down to the floor, drawing his knees to his chest and wrapping his arms around them.

"Shit, I'm sorry, Lane," Trey called softly.

He didn't answer, unable to articulate around the lump suddenly in his throat.

"Lane? Please."

Lane dropped his forehead to the top of his knees, shuddering.

"I… I'm sorry," Trey murmured.

Lane heard his footsteps as he walked away and wondered how the hell he would get through however long it would take to get the power on. He berated himself as tears trickled down his cheeks. *Stupid, stupid, stupid.* Wasn't what happened with Gregory enough for him? Wasn't hearing the boy he loved call him a disgusting faggot all the proof he needed no one could love him in return? Trey wouldn't be any different. He'd leave after he got what he wanted and Lane would be left to pick up the pieces again, on his own with no one to help him.

It took a while for him to gather the strength to get up. He stared at himself in the mirror, swollen lips and red-rimmed eyes, cheeks flushed with an emotion he couldn't identify. He turned on the water, bent down, and splashed water over his face. There was no way he could go out there like this. The urge to take a shower had long since fled his mind.

After he'd emptied his bladder, he washed his hands and tried to gather whatever wits he had left around him. He couldn't give in to Trey when all Trey wanted was a quick roll in the hay before he left at the end of next week. Before exiting the bathroom, Lane sent a prayer to whatever god might watch over him to let the roads be cleared and the power come back on quickly.

Sometime in the twenty minutes or so he'd been in the bathroom, Trey's parents had gotten up. He could hear Mrs. Jenkins talking as he approached the living room, except they weren't in there. He figured they must be in the kitchen and breathed a sigh of relief. Instead of joining them, he headed to the window to look outside. His heart dropped into his feet when he saw the street was still jam-packed with snow. He hoped they'd be cleared up later on in the day. Maybe the snowplow just hadn't gotten that far yet.

The soft sound of bare feet brushing over the wood floor caused his shoulders to tense and he crossed his arms over his chest, squeezing his biceps.

"Are you all right?"

Lane stiffened until it felt as though his spine would snap, and dug his fingers further into his arms. "I'm fine," he said flatly.

Trey sighed and moved closer. "I can't seem to do anything right when it comes to you. I can't even give you an excuse for what happened earlier other than to say I lost my head."

Lane heard sadness and something he couldn't identify in Trey's voice. He frowned, tilting his head forward to stare at the floor.

"If I promise to keep my hands to myself, *again*, will you please join us in the kitchen? Ma already fed Chloe, and if you don't, she's going to know something is wrong."

He hesitated.

"Please?" Trey said softly.

God, could he be any weaker, Lane thought to himself as he gave in and dropped his arms. He turned but couldn't look Trey in the eye as he walked past him. Trey trailed behind him, a constant heat at his back. Lane dredged up a smile he felt certain didn't quite reach his eyes when he walked into the kitchen, hoping Mrs. Jenkins didn't notice. Of course, she was a smart woman, and he saw her eyes narrow a bit at the edges, but she didn't say anything, for which he couldn't be more grateful.

They talked around him as he picked at the bowl of oatmeal she'd prepared. He heard Trey talking about some of the men at his job and one of his neighbors, causing the small crack already forming in his heart to break open wider. Trey had a life back in Texas, a place Lane would never belong, and one that wasn't Christmas Valley. Most people would question his desire to hold on to the town he lived in rather than consider moving to Dallas to possibly have something with Trey, but none of them would understand how much he couldn't trust himself to trust Trey.

CHAPTER 7

T REY'S ANKLE felt much better that morning, if his desire to dig out the front sidewalk of his parents' home was any indication. Lane warred with the urge to help and the side of himself demanding he remain as far away from Trey as possible. The kindness in him won out, and after he'd dressed in a pair of jeans two sizes too big for him, held up by a borrowed belt, and the long-sleeved shirt he wore the day they left his apartment, which Mrs. Jenkins had somehow washed without him knowing, he put on his boots and grabbed his hoodie and jacket.

When Trey came downstairs, he frowned at Lane. "You should stay inside where it's warm."

Lane ignored the bite of rejection and shook his head. "I want to help."

Trey studied him for a long moment and then sighed. "Let's at least see if Ma has an extra pair of gloves somewhere."

Minutes later Lane had a snow shovel in his hand and was working beside Trey to clear out the walkway to the street and the driveway. They wouldn't be able to drive until the snowplows came through, but this way it was already done. He saw others in the neighborhood doing the same thing, and the mindless activity soothed him as he dumped each shovelful away from the walk. Several times he bumped into Trey but merely apologized and continued to work. When they reached the end of the pathway, the muscles in Lane's arms quivered and he couldn't help his heavy breathing. Trey, of course, was barely winded. Lane made a face but started digging toward the cars.

"You can go inside and rest now if you want to. I can finish this up," Trey said.

Lane shook his head. "I'm fine."

He thought he heard Trey whisper, "Stubborn," but ignored the comment and kept digging. The crunch of the snow giving way to the shovel gave him a deep sense of satisfaction.

It wasn't more than a couple of feet into the mountain of snow between the walk and the driveway that he felt something hit his back. Lane jerked up and turned to stare wide-eyed at Trey, who smirked at him and casually tossed another snowball in the air, waiting to see what Lane would do.

"I can't believe you just did that!" Lane exclaimed. He scooped up a handful of snow and threw it at Trey. Some of it hit his chest, but it scattered as it flew through the air, making little to no impact. Trey raised an eyebrow, but instead of saying anything, he lobbed the one he held at Lane. Lane attempted to sidestep, but it grazed his arm.

The gloves were off and they started lobbing snow at each other. Trey had the clear advantage, having had many snowball fights in his life. Lane guessed Trey was going easy on him, though. He couldn't stop laughing, ducking behind mounds of snow to avoid whatever Trey threw his way. The longer they played, the more confident Lane became. He crafted each ball quick and sure, compressing it tighter as their fun continued, but it was the final snowball that hit Trey square in the face that ended their game.

Lane gasped in horror and rushed out from behind the barricade as Trey fell backward into a mound of white. "Trey!"

Lane almost slipped as he skidded to a stop next to where Trey lay. Trey's eyes were closed and he wasn't moving.

Lane dropped to his knees next to Trey. "Oh, my god, Trey. I'm sorry! Please be okay!" He leaned over and started brushing the snow from Trey's face, wincing at how red Trey's nose and forehead looked. "Trey," Lane pleaded and shook Trey gently.

Suddenly Trey reached up and grabbed Lane around the waist, twisting them until Lane lay beneath him. Lane gave a sound of protest, but it was cut off when Trey held a snowball he hadn't noticed before over him. "That wasn't very nice," Trey husked.

"I-I'm sorry," Lane stuttered, very aware of Trey's hard body on top of his. "I didn't mean to. Are you okay?"

Trey's eyes crinkled at the corner and one side of his mouth came up in a half smile. "All's fair in love and snowball fights, Lane."

He dangled the snowball closer to Lane's face. "You wouldn't," Lane protested, ignoring the comment about love.

Chuckling, Trey shrugged. "Maybe, maybe not. I'll make you a deal."

Lane swallowed. "What is it?"

"Go back inside and rest while I finish clearing the driveway or…." Trey lowered the snowball a bit more.

For half a second, Lane considered it and then said, "No."

Trey clucked his tongue a couple of times. "You really are a glutton for punishment."

Lane glared up at him. "I'm not going to sit around and do nothing while you're out here with an injured ankle."

He saw a slight hesitance in Trey's posturing, but it disappeared rapidly. Trey kept his word, but he didn't shove it in Lane's face as Lane expected, squeezing his eyes shut in preparation. Oh no. Trey chose to stuff it down the front of Lane's shirt. Lane gasped at the icy chill, eyes flying open to stare in shock at Trey, who had a wide grin on his face. He remained still for several seconds, absorbing what Trey had done and feeling the ice melt against his skin, sliding down his chest.

Instead of getting mad, Lane chose to get even. He grabbed as much snow as he could from beside him and shoved it up the back of Trey's leather jacket and under his shirt. Trey let out an exclamation of shock and sat up to fluff out his clothes in order to dislodge the ice. Seeing his chance, Lane squirmed out from under Trey and stood. He went to move around Trey but wasn't fast enough. Trey tumbled him down in the snow once more. Lane let out an "oomph" as he hit the hard white surface.

"The last person who did something like that didn't survive," Trey growled, eyes twinkling to show Lane he wasn't serious. Their faces were even closer to each other than before, and Lane noticed a small white scar at the corner of Trey's mouth and the dark flecks of brown hidden in the steel of Trey's irises.

"It was only fair," Lane wheezed.

Trey grunted. "Maybe so, but I can't let that trespass go."

Lane wriggled under Trey, attempting to get free once more. His movements caused Trey's eyes to darken to that liquid silver, and he halted, not really knowing what to do. He was tired of fighting it, but at the same time, knew he should hold strong against the only thing that lay in Trey's direction: pain.

"Lane?" Trey queried.

"Y-yeah?"

"Can I kiss you?"

Astonishment stilled any thought of getting away from Trey. Every other time Trey kissed him had been by surprise; to be asked made Lane question his resolve. "I-I…." He saw the disappointment in Trey's expression at his stuttering and his heart twisted. "O-okay," he whispered, silently answering the question to himself from earlier, if he could be any weaker. He couldn't hurt Trey no matter what his head demanded of him. Hurting Trey would be like hurting himself.

Trey's features softened and he brought one gloved hand up to stroke Lane's cheek. He trailed his thumb over Lane's lower lip before dipping his head down to lightly brush his mouth over Lane's. "I want to do what you ask of me, to keep my hands to myself," Trey rasped, "but you make it so hard by being so damn beautiful."

Heat flooded Lane's cheeks. Trey kissed him again once more, soft and sweet, and then stood, holding his hand out to Lane.

"Let's finish this."

Lane nodded and accepted Trey's offered hand. Trey didn't allow his hold on Lane to linger, and Lane tried to ignore how bereft it made him feel as he picked up his discarded shovel. They worked together for another hour or two to clear out a wide enough path for Trey's parents to back one of the cars out of the garage. Trey casually talked with him about various things while they shoveled: his favorite football team, the places he'd visited after college, and a few random topics. Lane listened attentively, wanting, needing to know more about Trey. He'd use everything he could to comfort himself after Trey left.

Mr. Jenkins came outside as they were close to finishing. "Would you boys like any help?"

Trey cut his father a sardonic look. "Thanks, Dad, but we're almost done."

Hiding a grin, Lane kept his head down and continued to shovel. They reached the end of the drive.

"We'll have to clear out some more once the plows come through, but we should be good," Trey said. "Thanks for helping me out."

Smiling, Lane replied, "You're welcome."

Trey placed a hand on Lane's lower back as they headed into the house. It made him feel… cherished.

Lane excused himself to use the bathroom once they'd taken off their jackets and boots. He needed a few minutes to clear his head. The more he was around Trey, the more he forgot to remember why it wasn't a good idea. He took several minutes to gather himself together, fiercely reminding his heart why it should remain locked away. Once he felt certain the traitorous organ had been thoroughly roped into place, he returned to the kitchen. Mrs. Jenkins had mugs of hot chocolate waiting for him and Trey.

"Where's Trey?" he asked and then could have kicked himself. Good Lord, hadn't he just beaten his attraction into place moments ago?

Mrs. Jenkins gave him a knowing look but kept her thoughts to herself. "He went upstairs to use the bathroom and grab a chessboard out of his room. He thought maybe you'd like to play for a little while."

Lane took a sip of his drink, savoring the warmth trickling through him. Before he could respond to her, Trey returned, said game in hand. He casually brushed his hand over Lane's shoulder, causing a heat in his lower belly that definitely wasn't the hot chocolate. He wondered if Trey even realized the gesture or if Trey would be the kind of lover who craved the unconscious connection with his partner. Then he stamped those thoughts right out of his mind. Thinking of Trey in any capacity as a lover wouldn't help his stubborn heart, which still refused to accept Lane's denial of what it wanted.

Trey set the board on the table and sank down, sighing as he picked up his mug. "I forgot how much work shoveling snow can be. You and Dad have Tal come help you out normally, right?"

"Of course, dear. Your father is not a spring chicken anymore, even though he likes to think he can still do the things he used to." Mrs. Jenkins set a plate of sandwiches between them. "Sorry I can't offer better fare while you're staying with us, Lane. Without my stove I'm a little lost on things more complicated than a salad or sandwich."

"I'm okay with anything," Lane protested. "Don't worry about me."

"Hopefully everything will be cleared up before the New Year's Eve party. I still have so much to do," she said.

"I am sure it will," Lane offered. He picked up one of the sandwiches and started eating. The sandwich tasted like ash on his tongue at the reminder of what would happen in less than a week. Trey would leave and Lane would be alone once more. He didn't finish the sandwich, placing the other half back on the main plate. "Have you seen Chloe?" he asked.

Mrs. Jenkins frowned at how little he'd eaten. "You need someone around to fatten you up, young man."

Lane flushed. "I'm not really a big eater."

"You're way too skinny," she admonished. He shrugged. "I think she's still in the living room, dear."

"Thanks," he said and escaped the kitchen. He had to search for a minute or two, but he eventually found her curled up in the basket of the faux tree near the doorway.

"You silly girl," he said affectionately and picked her up, holding her to his chest and petting her.

She purred, bumping her head on the underside of his chin. He chuckled and dropped a kiss on her nose.

When he looked up again, he saw Trey standing in the doorway, watching him. "You okay?" Trey asked.

Surprise held his tongue. He hadn't thought he'd been overly obvious. "I'm fine," Lane lied, forcing a smile.

Trey frowned. "You sure?"

"Of course. I'm always fine," Lane replied, hiding his face in Chloe's fur to avoid showing anything else.

"Okay," Trey said, not sounding at all reassured. "I thought you'd like to play a game of chess."

"I'm not very good."

"That's okay. Neither am I."

"Okay, sure."

Trey hesitated a moment before turning to go retrieve the chessboard. Lane settled Chloe on the ottoman while Trey set the board up. They'd only just started when Mrs. Jenkins joined them with some kind of knitting project. Lane had only played chess a few times with his father and in school. He didn't know strategy or anything, only what ways the pieces could move and which ones were what. It surprised him when he captured his first pawn, but as the game went on, he realized how Trey seemed to be moving his own pieces in ways that it seemed easier for Lane to take them.

"Are you letting me win?" Lane asked suspiciously.

"Why would I let you?" Trey asked, a little too innocent for Lane's liking.

Firming his lips, Lane sat back and crossed his arms, eyeing Trey. "I'm not a little kid you need to throw the game for, Trey."

"I'm not," Trey protested.

"Really? Then how come you've only got three of mine

and I have eight of yours?" Lane demanded. A sheepish look trekked across Trey's face. Lane gave a small growl. "Play for real."

"Okay, okay," Trey said, hands thrown up in a placating gesture.

Before they could get back into it, Mr. Jenkins appeared in the doorway. "Got some good news, everyone. Just spoke with Carl, our next-door neighbor," he added for Lane's benefit, "and he picked up on his CB radio that the snowplows were going to start up this afternoon and most likely be finished by around sundown. They'll be able to work on the power situation tomorrow!"

Lane's mood dimmed and he curled his hands into fists on his thighs. He knew he'd wished for this very thing to happen, but he hadn't realized just how much it would affect him. His stomach twisted and he had to battle the sadness pressing down on him. It wasn't like he could stop time. He knew that. Except... he'd really hoped to have more time.

He gave a strained smile when Trey called his name. Instead of saying anything, he moved one of his knights carelessly. It didn't matter when Trey took the piece or the next one, or even that Trey won the game. What mattered more than anything was how attached he'd already grown to the three people right there in the room with him. He knew he'd get to see Trey and Tal's parents from time to time in the restaurant, but somehow it didn't feel the same. He kept his mind away from the idea of Trey leaving because the very thought made his heart wrench with a pain almost twice what he felt when they took him away from Gregory.

He couldn't keep his mood up, and once they finished the game, he excused himself and went to the bathroom, where he fought to control himself. Tears pricked at his eyes and he fought to keep them under control. He'd cry when he got back to his apartment over Mrs. Johnson's garage. His lonely, cold, empty apartment filled with memories of Trey on his couch, in his bed. Lane shuddered and looked at himself in the mirror. Maybe staying in Christmas Valley wasn't a good idea. Maybe he needed to start over somewhere new again. The idea chafed. He liked Christmas Valley, the quirky people, the restaurant, the street names, and just everything about it. Yet he had no idea how he'd survive the depression creeping up from his soul at going back to being all alone again.

Over the last five years, he'd managed to forget what he didn't have: a family, friends, a home. Now… he knew what it would be like to belong to a loving, caring family again. He wasn't even sure moving to a new town would help him forget again either. Lane's eyes appeared bloodshot even though he hadn't cried, and he saw shadows darkening the normally light green irises. This, the pain in his chest, was why he chose to avoid people, to not get involved, even though his shyness kept most people away out of discomfort. He'd successfully avoided feeling as if his chest would cave in since Gregory had stomped on his heart, but now the emotion was back and worse than ever. The only way back to his sanity would be to cut all ties as soon as possible, to go home once the roads were cleared and the power back on, and bury the memories of the last three days under the rubble where his heart used to be.

A knock sounded at the door, startling him. "Are you all right, dear?" Mrs. Jenkins called.

Lane had to clear his throat a couple of times and he rubbed at his eyes before running a hand through his hair. He reached out and opened the door, forcing a smile on his face. "I'm okay," he said.

She gave him a worried look but seemed to accept his answer. "We're about to start up a game of Scrabble. Would you like to join us?"

"Sure," Lane replied, ignoring how much he'd rather not.

He remained quiet during their game, only speaking when needed. He saw Trey give him a weird look several times but chose to ignore it. Tension tightened his shoulders when he heard the snowplows approaching on their way down the street about halfway through the game. He tightened his fingers on the little square in his hand for a brief second as he began setting his word down, connecting to another Trey made moments ago. The end had begun.

Tal showed up about two hours later, close to sundown. He seemed surprised to see Lane there and even more so at Trey having stayed at Lane's on Christmas Eve. "I'm glad Trey was there to help!" Tal exclaimed, hugging Lane briefly, much to his chagrin.

Lane gave a strained smile. "I'm glad he was too."

That couldn't have been more of a lie. At least if he'd frozen to death in his apartment, it wouldn't have hurt as much as letting go of everyone. Everyone talked around Lane, Tal going on about how he'd been able to get caught up on some of his paperwork while holing up in the restaurant. Then he got into a full-on shouting match when Trey sheepishly revealed what had happened to Tal's truck.

Lane flinched and backed away, unable to stop the instinctive reaction. His shoulders hunched and he fought the urge to cover his ears.

"That's enough, boys!" Mrs. Jenkins snapped, rushing to Lane's side and wrapping an arm around his back. She was the only one to notice his response to the yelling. He leaned into her side, accepting the comfort.

Tal swore and approached Lane, bending down enough to peer into Lane's eyes. "I'm sorry, buddy."

Trey frowned. "What's wrong?"

Tal glanced at Trey, giving him some kind of signal to shut up, and then he looked back at Lane. "You doing okay?"

Lane bit his lip. He could feel sweat trickle down his face and swiped at it. "I'm fine," he whispered.

"You sure?" Tal asked, brushing a strand of hair back from Lane's face.

He nodded.

Tal gave a wry smile. "We wouldn't really hurt each other or anyone else, Lane. I promise. Just got mad at Trey for wrecking another of my trucks."

Lane frowned. "It wasn't his fault. It's mine."

"No, it's not," Trey huffed.

Tal ignored Trey. "Why do you think it's your fault?"

"Because I insisted on going home instead of staying at the restaurant like Trey said."

Perching one leg on the edge of the chair nearby, Tal leaned in closer and said, "That doesn't make it your fault. Trey just wanted to make sure you got home okay. In fact, it makes me feel better about why the truck was damaged in the first place."

Lane peered at Tal uncertainly. "Really? But... now you don't have your truck."

"It's just an object, Lane. It doesn't matter. I admit I was worried about you the last few days. You don't take care of yourself as much as you should."

"I would have been fine on my own," Lane mumbled.

"Maybe, but I'm happy you weren't by yourself."

Mrs. Jenkins gave his shoulders a light squeeze. "See? No harm done."

Trey still looked confused but also a bit... angry. Lane wondered what had happened to upset Trey. "I guess."

Tal smiled. "Good. Now I'm fairly certain your infamous Chloe is here somewhere, right? Knowing how much you adore that danged cat of yours, I doubt you left her on her own."

Lane grinned wide and bright, momentarily forgetting his sadness. "She's here!"

"Can I see her?"

Nodding excitedly, Lane dug her out of the same basket at the base of the faux tree and handed her to Tal, who exclaimed over her and how pretty she was. Lane unconsciously leaned on Tal as he also pet her, his free hand on Tal's arm. He'd gotten used to being around Tal, felt comfortable being close to him, the shy and damaged part of himself disappearing in the presence of Tal's kindness.

They were still talking about Chloe when a loud bang caused Lane to jump at least a foot off the floor. He looked around in surprise to find Trey gone and Mrs. Jenkins on her way out of the living room. She stopped to grab a jacket and then she exited the front door.

Lane frowned and looked at Tal. "What happened?"

Tal had a speculative expression on his face. "Not sure, buddy."

"Did I do something wrong?"

"You need to stop thinking like that," Tal reprimanded gently. "Everything is fine. I see you guys broke out the board games."

Lane nodded and started chatting about what they'd played and even revealed how he beaten Trey at Monopoly.

"The legend falls!" Tal chortled. "I'll be giving him hell for that for years."

"Don't," Lane protested. "I feel bad enough."

Tal snorted. "He needed his Monopoly ego taken down a few pegs! Congrats on being the one, Lane."

"I—"

"You did what the rest of us have been trying to do for almost three decades. Stop worrying about it. Besides, I doubt he's mad at you."

"I suppose," Lane said, unconvinced.

"No supposing about it, buddy. Let's see if we can start making something for dinner for everyone, okay?"

Lane nodded and followed Tal into the kitchen, still wondering what had caused Trey to walk out and why his mom followed. They were halfway through making more soup and sandwiches when Lane heard the sound of the front door opening. He tensed but continued putting cheese and turkey on bread. Tal had retrieved them from the box his mom placed outside the other day. Mrs. Jenkins joined them but Trey didn't appear. For some reason the whole situation made Lane uncomfortable, agitated. He hadn't done anything wrong. Had he? Why did he feel as though he'd kicked a puppy or something? He didn't even know why Trey went outside.

"Lane?"

When Lane looked up, he saw Mrs. Jenkins and Tal watching him, concerned and confused. He figured they must have called his name more than once. "Y-yeah?" he stumbled.

"I think we're good for sandwiches, sweetheart."

Lane glanced down to find he'd made at least ten sandwiches, way more than they'd need. He blushed and dropped the bread he held. "I-I'm sorry."

"No harm done," Mrs. Jenkins murmured and patted his shoulder. "Why don't you see if Ed and Trey are ready to eat, hmm?"

The only lights in the house were from the fire and candles Mrs. Jenkins had lit at some point. Lane couldn't look her in the eye as he fled from the kitchen, but he wasn't even sure he could look at Trey either.

He ran into Mr. Jenkins on his way to the living room and mumbled, "Dinner's ready," before changing course and darting toward the back of the house.

He didn't stop at the bathroom. Instead he chose to keep

going and went into the library. There was hardly any light except the moonlight streaming in the windows. Lane closed the door partially and sank onto the couch near the windows, bringing his knees up to his chest. He couldn't identify what had made him feel guilty, but something about Trey's abrupt departure earlier screamed at him, urged him to look at what he'd done. He frowned and rested his chin on top of his knees, arms wrapped around his legs. What had he done?

They must have realized he wasn't coming back because a good fifteen minutes had passed when he heard, "Lane?"

Lane stiffened.

CHAPTER 8

T REY PUSHED the door open wider, coming into the room. "Why are you sitting here by yourself?"

He shrugged one shoulder, not looking at Trey. Trey moved closer and sank down onto the wooden coffee table in front of the couch. "Everything okay?" Trey asked.

"Fine."

A soft sigh split the air and Trey slid from the table to the sofa. "I'm starting to know you better than that, Lane. 'Fine' is another way for you to say 'not fine,' but wanting someone to leave you alone."

Lane fidgeted but didn't respond.

"What's wrong?"

He hesitated, but agitation forced him to say, "What did I do?"

Trey sat forward a bit to be able to see Lane's face. "What?"

"What did I do?" Lane repeated.

"I don't understand. What do you mean what did you do?"

Lane ran one hand through his hair in frustration. "I don't know. I just… I feel guilty."

"About what?"

"I don't know!" Lane growled. "I didn't *do* anything."

"Then what is there to feel guilty about?"

"That's just it. I don't know," Lane replied miserably. "I…."

Trey placed his hand on Lane's shoulder, squeezing gently. "If you don't know, then there's certainly nothing to feel upset about. Why don't you come eat?"

"Not hungry," Lane muttered. He felt terrible for being so petulant, but he didn't know how to deal with what he couldn't identify. "Why did you leave?" he asked abruptly.

Trey didn't respond right away and Lane figured he wouldn't. When Trey did speak, it surprised Lane. "I got angry."

"Why?" Lane asked, peeking at Trey's shadowed face, the moonlight giving him an eerie look.

"In my whole life, I have never been jealous of my brother for anything. He's always been older, been able to drive before me, had more friends, even though I was popular in school. I've always been proud of him. Today, today I realized he had something I wanted so much."

Lane tilted his head in confusion. "What?"

Trey turned to look directly at Lane. "You."

Surprise struck through Lane and a shiver trickled down his spine. "What?" he repeated.

"You trust him. It was so obvious in the way you leaned against him, touched him. I wanted to be the one you trusted, the one you were eager to show Chloe to, the one who knew why our yelling at one another frightened you. When I saw how easily you accepted him saying the damage to the truck wasn't your fault after I'd been saying it for days, I got mad, at you, at him, but afterward I realized you don't have a reason to trust me. Aside from how I treated you at the beginning, I've done nothing except break your trust every time I've touched you, kissed you when you asked me not to."

"No!" Lane protested.

Trey gave him a droll expression. "You told me in your apartment nothing could happen, but since then I've done everything opposite, even knowing I wouldn't be here after New Year's."

Lane didn't know how to respond. He gave Trey a helpless look.

"I'm sorry, Lane," Trey apologized.

"It's okay," Lane said.

"No, it's not. I'll respect your wishes, Lane, from now on. I promise."

Something akin to despair wrenched Lane's heart and he had to force himself to bite his tongue, to not take back what he'd said the other morning. He knew what Trey said made sense, that it all did, but it still hurt and made his chest ache. What could he say without it leading to another disaster like it had with Gregory?

"Let's go eat, okay?" Trey said, standing and offering his hand to Lane.

Lane accepted the assist and felt like crying when Trey released him immediately. This was what he wanted, wasn't it? Then why did it feel as though he wouldn't ever be happy again? How could he even be this distraught over someone he'd only met a few days ago? Someone who was a good person, who cared about his family, made Lane feel cherished and so good inside, someone who'd helped with no thought of his own safety, only Lane's. Good Lord, he prayed he hadn't done something stupid like fall in love with Trey.

He followed behind Trey, silent and depressed. He barely ate a thing, his bowl of soup untouched, and only a few bites of one sandwich were all he could manage. When they finished, he retreated to his chair and ottoman, wrapping up in the blanket to fight off a chill, only the chill came from inside him. He needed to get away from everyone, to return to the real world and the knowledge of what he would never have.

T HE NEXT morning, after a restless night of little to no sleep, Lane woke to find the sun already up and Tal and Trey nowhere to be seen. He could hear Mrs. Jenkins in the kitchen and the fire still burning, but another sound also hit his ears: music. Christmas music?

Wait…. The knowledge that the power had been restored hit him full in the chest, and he bit back a sound of distress, then berated himself for being upset. He needed to go home to lick his wounds in private and be reminded of what he didn't have. Unwrapping himself from the blanket, Lane grabbed the few pieces of his clothing he wasn't wearing and made for the bathroom.

It didn't take long for him to wash off, dress, and return to the living room, where he put on his boots, folded the blankets, and set them, with the pillow, on the ottoman before returning *War and Peace* to the office shelves, the deck of cards forgotten on the coffee table. He would thank Mrs. Jenkins for her hospitality, put on his jackets, and, after picking up Chloe, leave. When he entered the kitchen, Mrs. Jenkins stood at the stove cooking eggs, and Lane's mouth watered at the smell of coffee. He'd been craving it but hadn't wanted to ask for it, figuring it would be rude. He rejected the urge to enjoy at least one cup. Once he was back home, he could indulge.

"Good morning, Lane," she greeted, bright and cheerful.

"Good morning. I see the power is back on."

"Yep, about thirty minutes ago. I'm surprised you didn't hear our cheers."

"I didn't."

"Have a seat, sweetheart. Eggs will be finished in just a few moments. We're going to try and salvage what's left of our Christmas today by opening presents, and have our missed dinner."

"If it's all the same to you, Ellen, I'd like to get Chloe and go home. I appreciate everything you've done for me. It was awful nice of you to accept me in even though you don't know me."

"What? You need to eat breakfast first," she chided, sliding an omelet onto a plate. "Here," she said, trying to hand it to him.

"Thank you, but I'm okay, really. I just need my own clothes and stuff."

She frowned and set the plate on the counter. "You don't have to rush off."

"I know, and I thank you for that, but I really just want to get back to my apartment," he insisted.

"Tal and Trey should be back any minute. They can take you."

"It's not that far. I can walk." He moved to her side and impulsively gave her a hug. "Thank you," he mumbled into her shoulder, squeezing with as much strength as he could muster before stepping back.

"You are welcome here any time you'd like, Lane. I really wish you'd wait for one of the boys to take you home."

Lane gave her a forced smile and shrugged. "I'm happy for the walk. Been doing nothing except sit around for the last several days. Not used to it."

She followed him to the hallway and watched him pluck Chloe out of the basket at the base of the tree and place her in his hoodie, zipping it up to protect her from the cold. Once he'd pulled his other jacket on, he opened the door, and Mrs. Jenkins pursued him out onto the porch. Lane stopped, noticing the end of the driveway had been cleared again after the plows came through, and how the endless sea of white was broken up by the dark asphalt of the road. They'd cleared it up quick.

He firmed his resolve and went down the steps. "Thank you again for everything."

"It wasn't any imposition, Lane. Please come to the New Year's Eve party, okay?"

"I'll try," Lane lied.

He turned his back on her and started walking. His breath crystallized the instant it hit the air and his fingers were already frozen through. He stuffed them into his pockets, seeking the socks he'd worn over them the other day. God, had it only been three days? Why did it seem like a lifetime, then? Lane smiled without humor and kept up a steady pace, shoulders hunched. Chloe shifted inside his hoodie and Lane soothed her, murmuring nothing in particular.

About halfway home, the sound of tires squealing on the wet asphalt caused his heart to leap into his throat and his breathing to double. His eyes widened and he jumped backward, his back hitting a snowbank. Then he heard, "Get in the car, Lane," in that familiar tenor.

Lane managed to get his heart rate under control. "I can walk," he protested and resumed walking.

The car shot ahead of him by a dozen yards and then Trey was out of the vehicle, stalking up to him. Trey grabbed hold of Lane's shoulders and shook him lightly. "You are so damn stubborn!"

Frowning, Lane stared at the road. "I don't want to cause anyone trouble."

"It's more trouble for you to leave without saying anything," Trey growled. "Ma thinks she did something to make you upset! Why… why did you just leave?"

Frustration and hurt resounded in Trey's tone, causing

shame to burn through Lane. Then he reminded his errant heart why he left in the first place.

"Why?" Trey repeated, harsh and rough.

"Because it's too damn hard," Lane burst out, covering his mouth with his hands after. He hadn't meant to say anything, and he didn't swear. His parents had never liked it and taught him the same.

"What's too hard?" Trey asked, voice softer now.

"Be-being around you, your family. Seeing what I don't have and never will," Lane whispered.

Trey remained quiet. All Lane could hear was their combined breathing in the early morning air. Most people hadn't roused from their homes yet. "You have a family, Lane," Trey finally said. "Ours. We care about you. All of us."

Lane looked up at Trey, sadness etched on his heart and face. "I don't have anyone."

Trey tightened his grip on his shoulders for a couple seconds. "Just… get in the car, Lane."

Instead of arguing again, Lane climbed into the front seat of a light blue station wagon. Trey joined him and put the car in drive. The trip to Lane's apartment was made in silence. When they pulled up to his front steps, Lane put his hand on the door and then hesitated. "Tell your mom I'm sorry. I didn't mean to upset her."

He opened the door and was halfway out when Trey stopped him. "Lane?"

Stopping, he waited for Trey to continue, but disappointment reigned when all Trey said was "I'll see you at the restaurant this afternoon. Tal wants to reopen as soon as possible."

"Sure," Lane said listlessly.

He shut the door and waded through the snow to his steps. Maybe Mrs. Johnson had a shovel he could borrow to clear out his walkway and the bottom of the stairs, he thought inanely as he listened to the car drive away, taking Trey with it.

Tears stung his eyes as he climbed the steps carefully. Once he unlocked his door and set Chloe down, Lane collapsed and started crying, no noise, just big, wet tears and shoulders shaking, silent and broken.

After he'd gathered himself, the first thing he did was turn on the radiator and kick off his boots. He changed out of his clothes for new, dry ones and made a carafe of coffee. Everything in his fridge would have to be gone through and some stuff thrown out, no doubt spoiled with the long drought on electricity. He'd figure that out later.

He needed to get to the restaurant and help Tal set up. People would most likely have gone stir-crazy sitting around their houses for days. That idea was confirmed when he left his apartment and there were already cars driving around slowly and people walking the roads. Lane returned the waves of some of the regulars from Tal's as he put one leg in front of the other, ignoring the deep ache inside him. He'd lived through it more than once. He could do it again.

Except… this time his heart didn't feel in it, and it took every ounce of strength he could muster to continue acting like it. Trey ignored him whenever it wasn't necessary for them to talk during the afternoon and evening hours up until closing. Lane didn't really understand it, but maybe Trey had decided Lane had been right. He was too much trouble.

At closing time Lane remained behind to finish cleaning up, setting the dishwashers and prepping some stuff for the next day. Trey never joined him as he did before the blizzard. He trudged home wearily, dejected and sad, to his empty apartment, feeling even more so now he'd experienced those three days with the Jenkinses.

The pattern continued until New Year's Eve. Tal closed up early that night. "Are you coming to the party, buddy?" Tal asked as he locked the back door. Trey had already gone on to their parents' house to help them prepare the food and set up.

"I don't think so. Not really in the mood," Lane murmured, starting to walk away.

"Lane?"

He stopped.

Tal approached him, placing one hand on his shoulder. "I don't really know what happened between you and Trey, but whatever it is, don't let it damage the progress you've made."

Lane gave him a confused look. *Progress?*

Tal sighed and reached up to brush back a strand of Lane's hair from his cheek. "In the six months you've been here, Lane, you've come so far out of your shell, and all I see is you retreating back into it now. Something changed while you were staying with my parents, and it wasn't for the better. I wish you would talk to me. It's not good to bottle everything up inside."

Tal had tried more than once since Lane returned to his apartment to get Lane to open up about what happened, but Lane couldn't talk about it. Every time he even thought about it, his eyes welled up, a bit like right then, to his horror. Lane shut his eyes and turned his head away from Tal. "I'm fine."

He heard Tal mumble something about Trey and a particularly nasty swearword.

Lane shivered and stepped back from Tal. "I'm all right, Tal. I'll see you tomorrow, okay?"

"We're closed on New Year's Day," Tal reminded him, not pushing the issue any further.

"Oh, right." Lane wanted to scream. He didn't want to sit around and do nothing except think about Trey, about the things he couldn't have. "I'll see you the day after, then."

"I hope you'll come to the party tonight, buddy. It'd be good for you."

"Maybe. I'll think about it." Lane knew he wouldn't. He was going to curl up with a book, a cup of coffee, and his cat, trying hard to distract himself from thinking about Trey.

Lane headed home, ignoring everything around him save for when he needed to cross the street. Mrs. Johnson called a greeting to him as he started up his steps. "Not going to the party, Lane?" she asked.

"No, Mrs. Johnson."

She frowned. "You're a young man, Lane. You should be out having some fun."

"I'm okay, Mrs. Johnson." He didn't give her a chance to keep asking questions or say anything else, darting into his apartment and closing the door.

He went about getting ready for his evening alone with his books, ignoring the memories of Trey on the loveseat and in his bed. Lane couldn't allow those thoughts in or he'd end up crying like he had every night. He needed to get past this never-ending cycle he'd found himself in for the last several evenings.

Chloe meowed at him as he fed her and then changed his clothing for comfortable sweats and a T-shirt, putting on new socks as well to keep his feet warm. After he attempted halfheartedly to eat dinner, he put away his leftovers and drained the mug of coffee he'd made. Chloe chased one of her jingle balls around the floor while he chose which book he wanted to read from the few on his shelf. For the next couple of hours, he lost himself in the world of dragons and brave knights, wanting to escape to a place other than his own.

The sound of a fist on his door caused him to jump and his heart beat fierce and hard at his rib cage. Lane set his book down and climbed off the bed. When he opened the door to a scowling Trey, his chest tightened and his stomach did a dangerous flip-flop. "Trey?"

"You didn't come," Trey growled.

Lane wrinkled his nose at the smell of alcohol on Trey's breath. "I didn't."

"Why?"

Shaking his head, Lane stepped back and urged Trey into his apartment, shutting the door behind him. "You know why."

"I don't," Trey argued, flopping down on Lane's sofa.

"You do. It's why you've avoided me the last few days," Lane muttered.

Trey glared at Lane, who stood fidgeting near the foot of his bed. "You made me."

Lane raised an eyebrow, stunned at Trey's words. "What do you mean I made you?"

"You said I didn't care about you."

"And ignoring me is supposed to convince me otherwise?" Lane didn't understand Trey's logic. He frowned. "How much have you had to drink?"

Trey waved his fingers as though Lane's question was irrelevant. "Just tell me why."

"Why what?" Lane said, frustrated.

"Why didn't you come to the party?"

Lane had no idea how to deal with a drunk Trey. He ignored the bad memories of foster homes caused by the scent of alcohol and the almost belligerent Trey. "I didn't feel like it."

"Because I'm there?" Trey demanded, lips pouting.

Sinking down onto the corner of his bed, Lane rubbed at his face with both hands. He glanced at the clock and saw it was just after ten. "Why are you here, Trey?"

Trey blinked at him. "Because you weren't there."

He said it so easily, as if it were the most obvious thing in the world. Anger began to mix in with the sadness and Lane gritted his teeth. "You have barely said a word to me in four days. Why should I have come?"

Trey dropped his gaze from Lane. "I didn't know what else to do."

"What?"

"You didn't even care how much you hurt me," Trey continued, ignoring Lane's words. "You just shoved a knife in my chest and twisted it."

Lane couldn't have been more confused. "What are you saying?"

Trey stood abruptly and paced in front of Lane. "I tried for days to ignore it, to forget it, but I couldn't. I know it's not possible, but there has to be a way. I mean, others have done it, why not us? I can fly in whenever I'm on a break at the station, and you can come visit me in Dallas."

Lane's mind whirled as what Trey was saying sunk in. He stared openmouthed at Trey. "Trey?"

"People do it every day, right? I—" He stopped talking and pacing to turn and look at Lane. "What?"

"What are you talking about?"

Trey strode to Lane and yanked him up from the bed into his arms. "This," Trey rasped before covering Lane's mouth with his.

Astonished at first, Lane could only stand under the onslaught of Trey's wet, alcohol-flavored kiss. As the kiss went on, Lane opened his mouth and allowed Trey the access that, if the groan that rumbled in Trey's chest was any indication, he seemed to hunger for. Lane brought his hands up and placed them on Trey's waist, digging his fingers into the jacket Trey still wore. Trey tightened his arm around Lane while Trey raised his other hand to cup Lane's cheek, rubbing his thumb over the smooth skin in a caress. Lane sighed, giving in entirely, no longer wanting to fight what he desperately desired.

Trey guided them down to the bed, never relinquishing the kiss or his hold on Lane, merely bringing them closer together, if that was even possible. Lane's senses swam with everything Trey; his nostrils breathed in the scent of Trey's skin, he dug his hands under Trey's jacket to touch the warmth of Trey's back. Trey growled and released Lane long enough to remove the jacket and the long-sleeved shirt he wore beneath it, then yanked Lane's T-shirt over Lane's head. Lane gasped when he found himself suddenly pressed to a bare-chested Trey.

"Trey," he whimpered.

The heat of Trey's skin seemed to almost burn against his. Lane couldn't stop his moans as Trey nibbled and kissed along his jawline to his ear and down to his throat. A sharp pang spiraled up from Lane's groin when Trey sucked in a bit of flesh at the base, hard. Lane slid his hands along Trey's broad shoulders and along his back, wanting to touch him more than anything he'd ever wanted before. Trey laved the bruised flesh with his tongue and then sucked at it again, no doubt leaving a mark everyone would see the next day. Somehow Lane didn't care, even acknowledging the embarrassment he'd experience when others saw it, but the joy of knowing how it got there would far outweigh everything else.

When Trey latched on to his nipple, Lane arched his back, letting forth a sound of pleasure. He buried his hands in Trey's hair, stroking through the thick locks with abandon. Trey did not linger at his nipples. Instead he rolled Lane to his back and continued down Lane's chest, along his abdomen to the top of his sweatpants, licking and kissing as he went. The wet swirl of Trey's tongue over and into his belly button caused Lane's penis to throb and weep, dampening the front of his pants. He'd never experienced any of this. Gregory always rushed, sometimes even hurting Lane in the process, but Lane hadn't known any different. There were never soft touches, light kisses, or gentle licks over Lane's entire body, nor had Gregory made Lane feel as though he were the only thing that mattered.

Lane grabbed for Trey's hands when Trey started to pull down Lane's pants. Trey looked up at him, pressing a kiss to Lane's lower belly. "Trust me," Trey husked.

Hesitant, Lane released Trey to do as he pleased, shutting his eyes as his weeping length caught on the edge of his pants before sliding free of its confines to brush along Trey's cheek. Lane bit his lip, only to release a shuddering cry at the first gentle swipe of Trey's tongue over the tip. His stomach clenched and he twisted his fingers in the bedsheets around him, panting as Trey repeated the same move over and over, but it was the moment Trey engulfed his entire member into his mouth that Lane would never forget.

"Oh God, Trey," he keened, tossing his head from side to side.

Trey hummed, sending shock waves straight through to Lane's testicles. Faster than he'd ever thought possible, Lane could feel himself ready to come.

"Trey," he pleaded, pushing at Trey's shoulders, "I… oh… please."

Lane shattered, arching his back from the bed once more, hips thrusting of their own accord. If Lane could have seen himself right then, he'd have died of embarrassment at how flushed he looked and how needy he sounded, but all he could do was lose himself in the heat of Trey's mouth and the steady contractions of his sac as he spilled every ounce of essence down Trey's throat. When he could open his eyes, Lane realized Trey had moved up beside him on the bed and was holding him and stroking his hair.

He blushed, burying his face in Trey's chest. Trey

chuckled and kissed Lane's forehead. "So beautiful," Trey murmured.

A hard bulge dug into Lane's belly and Lane reached down to cup Trey through his jeans. This part he knew. Gregory had taught Lane how to please him. Except Trey caught Lane's hand and brought it back up to his chest, holding it over his heart.

"Not tonight," Trey rasped.

Disappointment and hurt speared Lane and tears burned behind his eyes.

"Stop," Trey growled low. "I want to more than you could ever possibly understand, Lane, but I want you to know I want more than sex with you. When I leave tomorrow, I don't want you to think this means nothing to me."

Lane looked up at Trey, searching his face for dishonesty, and saw nothing except openness and affection. His heart tripped a beat and his breath hitched. He gave a small smile and nodded, burrowing against Trey and sliding his arm around Trey's waist.

"Di-did you mean what you said?" Lane managed.

"People do long distance all the time, Lane. We'll see each other as much as we can and we'll talk as often as we can. Okay?"

Happiness spread through Lane and he pressed his mouth to Trey's chest, above Trey's heart. A shiver trickled through Trey and Lane felt the heady rush of power come over him at the knowledge just how much he affected Trey. He did it again, this time openmouthed. Trey made a small sound, one Lane wanted to hear more of. When Lane moved down to Trey's nipple, sucking heatedly, Trey grunted and cupped the back of Lane's head.

"Lane," Trey warned, "stop."

Lane pulled away to look up at Trey. "I-I want to," he murmured.

Trey hesitated, then asked, "Are you sure?"

"Yes," Lane said without guile or uncertainty.

In answer Trey relinquished his hold on Lane's hand, and Lane took that as his answer to begin exploring Trey's body. He ran his palms over Trey's broad shoulders, savoring the feel of warm skin, along Trey's defined collarbone, and the muscular pectorals below. Trey's nipples were stiff nubs in light brown discs of color on tanned skin. The hiss Trey gave when Lane glided his hands over them made Lane smile shyly.

He couldn't help but be fascinated at the differences in their bodies. Gregory was taller and more muscular but nothing like Trey. Lane berated himself for thinking of Gregory again. He was here with Trey; nothing else mattered. Making a conscious decision, Lane banished Gregory from his thoughts, swearing to himself never to allow his past lover to enter into his thoughts while with Trey. Comparing the two of them was like night and day, and fruitless.

Lane reached to open the button and fly on Trey's jeans, separating the fabric. Trey wore black briefs underneath, his hard length causing a large bulge beneath them. He caught his breath when he freed Trey from the confines of his clothing. Trey was big, bigger than any he'd seen before. He bit his lip in nervousness.

"You don't have to do anything you don't want to," Trey said softly, running a hand down Lane's arm.

Shoring up his courage, Lane grasped Trey's penis. The shaft felt so hot it seemed to almost burn the inside of his palm. Trey moaned and instinctively thrust up through Lane's hand. Lane stroked him, loving how much pleasure he brought to Trey by such a simple act. He continued to caress Trey as he moved down until he was face to, well... head with Trey's member. The loud groan Trey released when

Lane flicked his tongue over the well-defined knob sent heat straight to Lane's groin. He swirled around the tip before sucking it into his mouth.

"Oh fuck," Trey panted, sliding one hand into Lane's hair.

If Lane's mouth hadn't been full, he might have laughed, but he concentrated on swallowing as much of Trey as possible. It would take time to take all of Trey, but he managed to encase two-thirds of Trey before gagging. Lane backed off to breathe for a second. He fondled Trey's sac, rolling it gently between his fingers as he suckled at Trey. The thick vein running the length of Trey's shaft pulsed and Lane followed the tantalizing throb with his tongue, relishing how good Trey felt.

Lane had no idea how long he pleasured Trey, but he knew the moment Trey reached the edge. Trey tightened his hand in his hair and he tried to pull Lane free, but Lane resisted, sucking harder.

"Lane!" Trey cried out, jutting his hips forward, length twitching as he came, spilling his come into Lane's mouth and down his throat. Lane felt the shudders wracking Trey's body as each spurt flooded his mouth, and swallowed as quickly as he could, but some trickled out, trailing down his chin. Trey tasted like heaven, heady and amazing. Lane knew he would never get enough of it.

When the last of Trey's essence had stopped and the only thing left were the shivers racing through Trey, Lane cleaned off his chin and returned to his original place, burying his face against Trey's sweaty chest.

Trey wrapped his arms around Lane, gathering him close, still panting. "God, Lane… that was…."

Lane smiled into Trey's chest but didn't respond, closing his eyes. Doubt nudged him, though. Would Trey remember all of this in the morning? After all, he'd been drinking all night.

Something must have given away his thoughts because Trey said, "Stop whatever negative thoughts are going around inside that gorgeous brain of yours."

The whole situation reminded Lane of the night they were snowed in and he almost laughed. Almost. "Ar-are you sure?" Lane asked.

Trey knew what he meant. "Never been more certain about anything in my life, baby."

The endearment made Lane feel giddy. "Okay," he whispered.

Loud popping sounds came from outside right then and Lane jerked, eyes flying open.

"Shh, it's just fireworks, baby. It means it's midnight. Happy New Year, Lane."

A smile crossed Lane's lips and he stretched up to kiss Trey. "Happy New Year."

CHAPTER 9

ix months later....

LANE FINISHED clearing off the table a family had just vacated, wiping down the surface. He glanced at the clock, anxious for the evening to be over. Trey was flying in that night for an extended weekend and he couldn't wait to see him. They hadn't seen each other in over a month, although they talked almost every day.

Trey had kept his word after New Year's. Even though it hurt to see him leave, the same night Trey had called him from Dallas and they'd talked for hours. Lane had finally told Trey everything about his past, including Gregory. Not all at once, of course, but over the six months, he'd let go of the horrors holding him back.

He now had a cell phone under Trey's plan despite all of his protests. Trey had gotten frustrated when there was a week of them playing phone tag. Lane had never been able to afford one. Trey had mailed it to Lane at the restaurant and insisted he keep it. It had taken time for him to learn how to use the different functions, but eventually he could use the video conference with Trey, and it was so good to see Trey's face whenever they talked now. He flushed as he remembered a few particularly heated sessions together, and the memory sent heat spiraling to his belly. The first time Trey had returned for a visit, they had consummated their relationship entirely. Lane squirmed as he thought of how Trey had felt inside him.

After New Year's the Jenkinses carried through on locating him a new place. He now had a quaint little cottage over on Comet Avenue behind the house of Joe Thompson, the man who owned the hardware store. Lane loved it and had really made it his own, finally knowing he wasn't going anywhere. It was a separate cottage-style house with a small kitchen, living room, one bedroom, and a bathroom. There was a fireplace and central heating, which Lane couldn't believe the man, Mr. Thompson, rented to him at such a cheap price. Somehow he had a feeling the Jenkinses had a hand in that.

Two months into their long-distance relationship, Lane went to Dallas to stay with Trey for a week. He met Trey's friends and saw the firehouse Trey worked at. The city itself was beautiful but way too big for Lane to consider ever calling home, a fact he kept to himself. They still hadn't discussed what would happen long-term. Lane knew he didn't want to leave Christmas Valley, but he would consider moving if it meant he could be with Trey. He'd finally admitted, not to anyone except himself, that he'd fallen head over heels in love with Trey. He was afraid to tell Trey, having no idea if Trey felt the same way or if Trey would reject his feelings, so he remained silent, hoping someday Trey would come to love him in return.

Trey would be coming in late and had told him not to wait up. He had a key to Lane's little home and would let himself in. He'd told Lane he had a surprise for him, and Lane couldn't help wondering what it was. Maybe Trey had gotten the promotion at work he'd spoken about wanting. The clock seemed to be crawling at a snail's pace, and Lane wanted to scream at it to hurry up.

"Lane," Tal said from behind him.

Lane smiled and turned around, the smile dying when he saw Tal's face. Deep worry and sadness lined Tal's features. "Tal, what's wrong?"

Tal came closer and took Lane's hand, led him to a chair, and pushed Lane down into it before crouching in front. "I don't really know how to say this. I… shit." Tal shoved a hand through his hair and looked away. "Something's happened."

Lane frowned. "What do you mean?"

"There's been an accident. There was a fire. Trey got trapped inside."

Lane's heart stopped. A roaring filled his ears and he was transported back to the day eight years ago they told him his parents had been killed in a car crash. Nothing Tal said registered. Numbness settled over him and Lane stared at Tal.

"…hospital. Lane? Hey. Lane. Aw shit." Tal reached up and shook Lane's shoulders. "Lane, come on. Trey needs you."

Tears welled up. "I-is h-he a-alive?" Lane babbled.

"He's in intensive care at Baylor University Medical Center. They said he's… he's burned pretty badly."

"I need to see him," Lane sobbed. "I need to see him, Tal. Please."

"I know, buddy. I already booked us a flight out there, okay?" Tal rubbed Lane's shoulder.

"What about the restaurant?" Lane asked inanely, still in shock.

"Adam can handle it."

Tal had finally given in to the nagging from both his mom and Lane about needing to hire an assistant manager. There was too much work to be done and Tal couldn't do it all himself anymore. Adam Grant had just moved to town the week before to care for his ailing grandmother, a woman who'd lived in Christmas Valley for sixty years. Everyone knew Mrs. Harold Grant, a vibrant, caring sweetheart of a person to anyone she met. The whole town would feel her loss when she moved on.

"Okay," Lane murmured. "I… I need someone to look in on Chloe."

"I already called Joe. He said he'll take care of her. The flight leaves at three. Why don't you go home and grab some clothes. I'll pick you up in an hour and we'll head to the airport, okay?"

Lane nodded slowly, afraid any quick movement would shatter him. He stood and walked toward the back room to get his wallet and keys from his locker as he heard Tal call for Adam. Time seemed to slow down even further, and Lane could hardly bear not knowing what was happening with Trey. Tal had called his parents, who'd already arrived in Dallas ahead of them, but they knew about as much as Tal had already told Lane. Nothing mattered except getting to Trey. He needed to be with him. What if it was too late? What if Trey died before Lane could tell him how he felt or before he got to say good-bye, like his parents had? Lane ranged from crying silent tears to completely dazed and numb. Tal tried to keep him calm, but none of it helped.

When they finally arrived at the hospital, it was all Lane could do to hold himself back. The moment he saw Trey in the bed, machines hooked up and bandages on part of his body, Lane started sobbing all over again.

He rushed to Trey's side, carefully picking up Trey's hand

and holding it to his cheek. "Don't leave," he begged. "Please don't leave me."

Mrs. Jenkins placed an arm around his shoulders as he stood there, tears streaming down his cheeks. "Why isn't he awake?" Lane choked.

"They have him in a medically induced coma, sweetie, so he can rest and heal. He has burns over 25 percent of his body."

Horror swept through him and Lane leaned down to kiss Trey's cheek. There was no damage to Trey's face that he could see, but he saw the bandages peeking through the top of the hospital gown. "Is he going to be okay?"

"The doctors say he'll be fine. He'll need a long time to recuperate and he will need surgery to repair some of the damage." Mrs. Jenkins patted his shoulder. "Visiting hours are almost over, Lane. I think we should go get some rest and come back tomorrow."

"I'm not leaving him," Lane growled, refusing to relinquish his hold on Trey.

"I had a feeling you wouldn't," Mrs. Jenkins said and pointed at a roll-away cot. "I told them you were his fiancé, dear. They don't typically allow nonfamily in ICU."

The idea of being Trey's fiancé struck Lane's heart hard and tears welled up again. He would love to be nothing else. Sniffling, he replied, "Thank you."

"I'm glad he found you, Lane. You've been good for him." She smiled affectionately at him and kissed his cheek. "If you need anything, call us, okay?"

Lane nodded and, without letting go of Trey's hand, pulled a chair near and sank down into it, staring at Trey's face as the others left. He laid his cheek on the bed and waited. A nurse came in at some point, checked some vitals, and then left without a word. Lane never looked away from Trey.

Night slipped into day and day into night. Trey's parents and Tal came to visit, sitting with both of them. Mrs. Jenkins brought Lane something to eat, but he refused, letting it sit on the small stand near Trey's bed. Trey's partner at the fire station and several of the friends Lane had met also came to visit. They offered their support to the Jenkinses and also Lane, who gave them a tremulous smile but never wavered in his watching over Trey.

The third day after his arrival in Dallas, Mrs. Jenkins came in with a cup of coffee for him and another sandwich from the cafeteria downstairs. "Lane Freeman, if you don't eat, I'm going to tan your hide with whatever handy item I can find," she threatened, holding out the sandwich.

None of the food she had brought the previous days was eaten. The only thing he'd had was coffee and some water, and the only time he left Trey's bedside was to use the bathroom. Dark rings circled his eyes and a three-day soft stubble dotted his chin and cheeks, but Lane could care less. He'd never been able to grow a full-on beard or mustache. His father had been pretty much the same way.

Lane rubbed at his eyes and accepted the sandwich, opening it and taking out half. He managed a bite, but it tasted like ash, and he could barely swallow around the lump in his throat.

Mrs. Jenkins touched his cheek and then sat down beside him. "Has he woken up at all?"

"No," Lane croaked, dropping the sandwich back into its packaging. He looked down at his lap. "I-I never told him."

"Told him what, sweetie?"

"That I-I love him."

Mrs. Jenkins gripped his hand and squeezed gently. "He knows, dear. He knows."

It wasn't until the following morning and after Lane finally fell into a fit of exhausted sleep at Trey's bedside that

Trey woke. Lane was dreaming about Trey and the last time they were together: the feel of Trey holding him, the peppering of kisses over his face, and the touch of Trey's hands on Lane's body.

"Don't leave me, Trey," he murmured.

"I'm right here, baby."

"I love you."

"I love you too, Lane."

Lane struggled through the cloud of sleep to find Trey staring down at him, an affectionate smile on his face. He startled. "Trey!"

"Hey, baby."

"Oh God." Tears welled up and spilled over. "I thought—"

Trey shook his head and cupped Lane's cheek. "Don't. I'm okay."

Lane leaned into Trey's touch, closing his eyes. "I was so worried."

"I know, baby." Trey rubbed his thumb over the sharp ridge of Lane's cheekbone. "You haven't been taking care of yourself," he admonished gently.

Flushing, Lane turned his head and kissed the inside of Trey's palm. He didn't care about anything except Trey being all right.

"So you love me, huh?"

Shock brought Lane's head up and his eyes flew open. Had he said something in his sleep? Trey had a wide smile on his face and Lane dropped his head back to the bed, groaning.

Trey chuckled and ran his fingers through Lane's hair. "I love you too, baby."

Lane remembered the tail end of his dream and realized he hadn't been dreaming it. "Trey," he sighed.

Before they could say anything more, the room became a flurry of activity. Doctors, nurses, and Trey's family flooded in, barring any chance for them to be alone. Trey would need to remain in the hospital for another few days for observation, but would be moved out of ICU now that he was awake. Lane never left Trey's side as they listed everything Trey would be expected to endure as he went through recovery. He would ensure Trey followed them to the letter.

It wasn't until Trey was in his own private hospital room and visiting hours were over that they were able to talk again. Trey beckoned Lane to climb onto the bed with him. "No! I don't think that's a good idea," Lane protested.

"Please?" Trey pouted.

"What if… what if I hurt you?" Lane asked.

"You won't. The only thing I want is to hold the man I love." Trey held out his hand again.

Lane hesitated but gave in and gingerly climbed onto the bed. Trey was still heavily dosed on pain meds, but Lane didn't want to cause him any further pain. Lane rested his head on Trey's unhurt shoulder, sighing at finally being held once more.

"I missed you," Lane whispered.

"I missed you too, baby." Trey sighed and kissed the top of Lane's head. "This definitely didn't turn out the way I planned it. I had this big weekend arranged and I wanted to tell you something. Besides the fact that I love you."

Lane shivered and kissed the edge of Trey's jaw. "It's okay. I'm just glad you're okay. Wh-when Tal told me, I-I didn't know what to do. I thought I had lost you and I was afraid I wouldn't get to tell you how much I love you."

Trey tightened his hold momentarily. "I have something to tell you. Remember I told you I have a surprise for you?"

Nodding, Lane replied, "You got the promotion you wanted?"

Trey chuckled. "No, baby. I got a new job."

"Really? Where? Are you still a firefighter?" Lane asked.

"Yes, I'm still a firefighter. I'm actually the new fire chief for the Christmas Valley Fire Department."

It took several breaths for what Trey said to sink in. When it did, Lane sat up and stared down at Trey. "Really?"

"Really, really," Trey teased, smiling, eyes sparkling.

"So you're moving back to Christmas Valley?"

Trey nodded. "I was going to tell you this weekend after I asked you to marry me."

Lane froze and stared openmouthed at Trey. Once again tears filled his eyes, but this time they were borne of happiness so deep Lane felt as though his heart would explode. "Marry you?"

"Will you, Lane? Marry me? Make an honest man out of me?"

"Yes," Lane breathed. "Oh God, yes."

Trey smiled and pulled Lane back down to him, kissing him breathless until Trey's body protested his actions.

Lane could hardly believe how much his life had changed in the last year. He had gone from being a nobody, alone, with no one to share his life with, to being a friend, a boyfriend, and now it seemed as though he would be getting the family he'd so wished for all those months ago. His heart swelled inside his chest, almost ready to burst out of his rib cage at how much love he felt in that moment.

If anyone asked Lane a year ago where he thought his life would end up, Lane could never have dreamt of so many wonderful things happening to him. He could hardly wait to return home with Trey and begin their life together. He wished he knew the name of the trucker who had left him behind in Christmas Valley so he could thank the man, because if he hadn't ditched Lane, Lane never would have met Trey and never would have known how amazing love could be. He snuggled closer to Trey and closed his eyes, safe in the knowledge tomorrow was theirs, and nothing could be more perfect.

Love freebies? Stop by J.R.'s website to subscribe for updates to receive a free friends to lovers novelette titled White Rain! Just enter your name and email address to subscribe! www.jrloveless.com

Looking for another hurt/comfort holiday romance? Try my novella Blue Christmas!

Christmas used to be a time of joy for me, but since my mother's death three years ago the holiday has lost all meaning, becoming nothing but a harsh reminder of what I've lost. I've become bitter and skeptical of everyone around me, and the cold aloofness has kept me from being hurt that deeply again. But this year the thought of yet another blue Christmas alone sends me on a path that will change my life forever. Trigger Warning: Attempted suicide.

A scarred young man jumping at shadows. A big-hearted, sexy cowboy providing him a safe haven. But is he able to trust his cowboy with his heart?

Love hurt/comfort contemporary romances? Try Touch Me Gently! Available on Kindle and Kindle Unlimited.

A NOTE FROM J.R.

Thank you for reading Love & Snowball Fights. If you enjoyed it, I would truly appreciate if you could let your friends know so they can also enjoy the relationship between Lane and Trey. If you leave a review for Love & Snowball Fights on the site in which you purchased the book, Goodreads or your own blog, I would love to read it. Please email the link to jrloveless@gmail.com

ABOUT THE AUTHOR

J.R. Loveless began her adventure in writing at the young age of twelve. Her foray into creating her own worlds and telling her characters' life stories was triggered by her own love of reading. She currently resides in South Florida with her dog and two cats, and by day works as a manager for a financial lending institute.

Her journey into gay romance began in 2005 when she began posting her original fiction on a forum for feedback and readers' pleasure. In 2010, a good friend urged her to submit to a publishing company, and the day she received the acceptance and contract was the best day of her life. Since then, she has been noted to be one of the most purchased audio books after Fifty Shades of Grey on Audiobook.com and received best gay romantic fiction for Touch Me Gently in the 2011 TLA Gaybies.

J.R. adores her fans and loves hearing from them.

Never miss out on an update or sale by subscribing to J.R.'s Website. As a thank you, you'll receive a free short novelette called White Rain about two friends who become lovers!

J.R.'s Blog

J.R.'s Facebook Reader Group

facebook.com/authorjrloveless

twitter.com/J.R.%E2%80%99s%20Twitter

instagram.com/jrloveless

amazon.com/author/jrloveless

bookbub.com/profile/j-r-loveless

goodreads.com/jrloveless